Alex in Rome

Alex in Rome

Tessa Duder

Houghton Mifflin Company

Boston 1992

Library of Congress Cataloging-in-Publication Data

Duder, Tessa.
   Alex in Rome / Tessa Duder, — 1st American ed.
      p.   cm.
   Summary: As a member of the New Zealand swimming team, fifteen-year-old Alex gets her first taste of independence as she faces the challenges of competition in the 1960 Olympic Games in Rome.
    ISBN 0-395-62879-2.
    [1. Swimming—Fiction.   2. Olympic Games (17th : 1960 : Rome,
Italy)—Fiction.]   I. Title.
PZ7.D8645Am   1992   91-41275
[Fic] — dc20   CIP
                  AC

Printed in the United States of America

AGM 10 9 8 7 6 5 4 3 2 1

Contents

Author's note

Alex in Rome could not have been written without the help of a number of people, especially:

The Literature Programme of the Queen Elizabeth II Arts Council, whose travel grant allowed me to undertake research in Rome, and Denise Almao, First Secretary of the New Zealand Embassy, for invaluable help while I was in Rome.

CONI, the Italian Olympic Games organization in Rome, where helpful library staff, especially Maurizio Bruni, allowed me access to printed material and to bear triumphantly away a video copy of the four-hour official film of La Grande Olimpiade, Roma, 1960.

D. Jack Lyons, life-long friend, for thirty years manager of the Olympic Pool, Newmarket, in Auckland, and a successful and influential swimming coach throughout; Piera Zigliani-Sexton; and Janice Webb, an Auckland singer and teacher much loved by her pupils and friends.

Staff members of the English Department of the University of Waikato, Hamilton, where I completed *Alex in Rome* during 1991 as Writer in Residence.

Though set in Rome 1960, this novel remains a work of fiction. No New Zealand swimmer competed at the Rome Olympics.

Sports historians will know that the medallists in the women's 100 metre freestyle event were Dawn Fraser of Australia, Chris Von Saltza, U.S.A., and Natalie Steward of Great Britain. These, and other outstanding swimmers of the Games — Murray Rose, Jon and Ilsa Konrads, John Devitt, and Lance Larson — are mentioned, as well as the previous New Zealand Olympians Jean Stewart and Marrion Roe, and some of the outstanding athletes of the Rome Games, including the New Zealand gold medallists Murray Halberg and Peter Snell.

Otherwise, all characters are fictitious.

The most beautiful pool in the world

Where . . . how to begin, eh Alex, when in Rome?

I turned over the last entry in my diary very firmly, a whole lot of gloomy stuff about crashing at Karachi airport, the Last Will and Testament of Alexandra Beatrice Archer aged 15 years 10 months, but we didn't crash, obviously, and we made it triumphal to Rome, she lives to swim another day . . . so, on a clean white slate . . .

Sat . . . my damn ballpoint wouldn't write properly . . . **urday, August** . . . **13, 1960.** I couldn't write properly, either. Teachers always complain about my handwriting but they'd have a fit at this. **2.30 p.m. Olympic Village, Rome, Ita** . . . Why has a large drop of water just trickled down the side of my long nose and plonked onto the empty page? Why is my hand shaking and even the date looks wrong?

Here's why, diary. Because I'm lying in bra and pants in stifling heat on a new bed in a new twin-bed room in the new Olympic village in Rome and somehow we've lost twelve hours and the dates *are* wrong. (My writing is really appalling, like a spider on the booze.) I thought we'd had Sunday in Karachi or Cairo or somewhere up at twenty thousand feet, but when we arrived it was still Saturday August 13th here and I am totally confused.

And now, more or less left to myself, stranded with a stranger in this hot, pink, and airless room, I'm about to let go another whole Niagara.

Copious tears for Maggie who is lying in a hospital bed hooked up to tubes of blood ten thousand miles away instead of being here sharing this room with me. And Andy whose gravestone I haven't yet faced up to visiting. For my fragile wee

1

Gran whose last bright smiling wave to me at the airport sent a shiver down my spine, and Mr Jack left behind because the officials back home think that coaches aren't all that important, though swimmers know better. For Mum and Dad because I know I've been hurting them for a long, long time and couldn't stop myself.

And yes, I'm crying for me too because after the long dismal winter, it's suddenly glorious hot summer and I'm here, after all, and I can compete in the Olympic Games, after all, and Maggie hasn't died and is going to live to swim another day too. Because I'm not used to feelings of such happiness.

Thankfully, my room-mate Zoe, a skinny high jumper from Wellington, has stripped naked, pulled her sheet up to her chin and gone straight to sleep, flat on her back, hands clasped across her chest like those medieval tombstones. Unlike a tombstone, she is snoring lightly. I hope it isn't a habit. The wooden shutters are making stripes of dusty heavy sunlight across the room. We've been told about these Italian afternoons, when the shops shut and the traffic crawls almost to a standstill and all sensible Romans retire inside to sleep or sit under a pine tree and drink wine.

Well, I'm not Roman and I've never been all that sensible at the best of times (you can ask my best friend Julia) and though I don't know whether I'm Arthur or Martha, laughing or crying, there's no way I can rest and only one thing I want to do now. One place I *must* go to remind myself who I am and why I'm here.

We had driven past the new Olympic pool in the cool, springy bus, on our way in from the airport. I think I was still in a state of shock, having just heard from some man from the New Zealand Embassy meeting us in the arrival lounge that Maggie was at long last getting better from her emergency peritonitis operation. *Also* that my name had been cleared of allegations that I'd unwittingly become a professional (modelling and therefore advertising swimsuits, would you believe?!) which I'm fairly sure was due to a nasty little scheme cooked up by Maggie's nasty mother to get me disqualified from the Games. My long winter and the journey to Rome have not been in vain.

2

Anyway, we thirty-nine supposedly fit but actually half-dead, very smelly athletes and twelve old officials were all put in this bouncy bus for the final leg to the Olympic Village. We drove too fast on the wrong side of a flag-lined motorway in a tide of tourist buses and peculiar cars and huge trucks with Italian names on the sides; along noisy tree-lined streets with trams and orange buses and motorbikes and scooters. The road signs, except for a few names like Roma, Napoli, Città del Vaticano, meant nothing. We jolted stop-start past terracotta buildings with brown shutters and wrought-iron lamps, over cobblestones and flagstones, through piazzas and around fountains with water streaming over streaky white marble horses, male bodies, animals, shells, all curving and wet and cool. We swung around the archways of the *actual* Colosseum, and then looked down onto jagged pillars and ruins which I guessed to be the Forum, the real Forum where Julius Caesar got stabbed in the back, and above, the brick ruins on the Palatine Hill where the Emperors lived. I wanted to get out there and then, and walk among them, touch, smell, feel, listen to them. When those stones fell over, New Zealand had no people in it, only birds. Then this amazing white, well hardly just a building, more a monstrous wedding cake, and streets hung with Olympic flags and banners and the pavements packed solid with tourists, here for the Games. To see us. We looked down on cheerful umbrellas, outside the Caffè di this and the Ristorante di that, where relaxed-looking people sat at tables, drinking and eating and watching the world go by. (Why can't we sit outside like that at home, in summer? Tables and umbrellas in Customs Street, why not?). This terrible sight broke the silence in the bus. 'I could use a beer,' one guy behind me said mournfully, followed by 'I'll say!' and a few longing grunts. I could use one myself.

Stopped at traffic lights, I felt even more like someone dropped in from outer space; closer, these people were so brown, so fit-looking, so brightly, elegantly dressed, so exactly Roman. They belonged. We flew alongside dusty green parks and across a white bridge decorated with statues, tall ornate lamp-posts, more flags, the greenish river below; alongside the river, till someone cried out loudly, 'There's the pool, Alex,' but

3

I was on the wrong side of the bus and caught only a glimpse of the scaffolding of some huge stands amongst the pines. 'There's the stadium, folks!' several cried, louder still, because whatever our sport, every single one of us would march there in the opening ceremony. So we all stood up to see a big white piazza bounded by hedges, flagpoles, trees, flat brick buildings, a blinding white obelisk. The bus screeched right to cross the river again, but through the back window we could see at the far end of that white piazza the curving flanks of a gigantic stadium sitting under a tree-covered hill. I was near the back of the bus. When I turned around to sit down again I could see pairs of male faces still peering over the green seatbacks, their eyes bulging. Apart from a few people, like the long-distance runner Murray Halberg, most of us were first-timers to any sort of Games, and all of those faces looked utterly dead scared to me. Then I thought of that immense stand of seats above the pool, and a familiar feeling of dread mixed with pleasure stirred in the pit of my stomach. Another five hundred yards under more flagpoles and between pale brown buildings and we were there, outside the main entrance to the village.

We were all too totally exhausted to speak. We hauled ourselves out of the bus, claimed our travel bags and suitcases weighing no more than 35lbs; stood around, dimly aware of our black blazers being eyed by very healthy-looking athletes sauntering past. We tried to listen to yet more instructions, were given identity cards, handbooks, maps of the village, maps of Rome, sightseeing brochures, timetables, programmes, more instructions as if we weren't saturated already. We bumped our bags off to the allocated apartment block, up the stairs, found our room and bliss! a bed of my own for the next three weeks. Fling open the orangey shutters, discover a view of parched brown grass between us and the next identical apartment block, unlock my bag, fling off clothes, collapse on bed. Truly horizontal. Aaaaaaah.

But I lay there, twitching, tingling all over, tight as a drum, trying not to listen to Zoe's complaints about the unbearable heat and shampoo leaking all through her suitcase and sore calves and swollen ankles and no team physio to massage them back into jumping shape. I tried to write my diary but that was no use, it just ended up making me want to cry.

While Zoe snored, I tried doing some silent sit-ups on the wooden floor, press-ups, some old ballet pliés and développés. Nothing worked. My body said I needed water, that stretching, soothing, powerful rhythm that is so ingrained in me.

My whirling mind was saying: something is going to happen to me here, in Rome, and not just the Games. Isn't that *enough*, Alex? No, something else, something *else*, much more mysterious, delicious, unpredictable, scary too . . . there's such music here, and singing and ruins and paintings and churches . . . something, waiting . . .

The pool hadn't been so far away, when we drove past. Walking distance, surely. Mrs Churchill had pleaded for an hour's rest, *please* Alex, before we go over to the pool. Even behind the closed door, next room to mine, I could hear her snoring tunefully, out for the count. I had no idea where to find Mr Upjohn, somewhere in the men's quarters. It crossed my mind that my two guardian angels might not approve, but it was broad daylight and only just down the road and I just couldn't wait.

It felt just like being a new chum, the first day at school, only more so. Being siesta time there were only a few athletes out and about, in twos and threes, in very brief shorts or wondrous strange track suits of every possible colour. I felt very alone, but I'd got used to that, this past year. I tried to look as though I knew exactly where the gate was, much too nonchalant and/or busy to say hullo, even to a tall girl in a green and yellow track suit with AUSTRALIA written all over it and therefore someone who spoke English, even possibly a swimmer, even possibly friendly.

At the gates set into a high wire fence, like a prison, a couple of guards looked me sleepily up and down, and lengthily examined my identity card. 'New Zealand . . . ah, la Nuova Zelanda.' They both had droopy eyes and moustaches, evil grins and guns hanging from their belts. *Guns*. . . to keep the women in or the men out? I'd never seen a gun up close in my life, let alone on a policeman. 'Si,' I said somewhat haughtily because I didn't feel like trying out my fifty words of Italian yet. 'Excuse me.' Smirking at me, he held onto my card a fraction longer than was necessary. 'Permesso,' I said firmly. I saw a grinning laconic gesture which said *be my guest*, and felt their eyes following. We'd heard about bottom-pinching Italian men too. I began to wish fervently that I'd put a skirt on, however crumpled, not this sleeveless top and pale blue shorts — and brought a hat.

The roads were wide, with few trees for shelter from the baking sun, and not much traffic, just a few orange buses and motor scooters. By the time I reached the bridge I was wet all over and longing for shade, but this was the Tiber I was crossing, on the Ponte Duca d'Aosta, whatever that meant. Beneath me was the Tiber of my Latin books, Romulus and Remus, Rome beginning as a collection of mud huts by the river, Tarquin the Proud, the Punic Wars, Hannibal and his elephants, and Augustus and Nero and Rome burning and all that.

Ye gods! Miss Binning, I remember! You would be a happy woman if you knew how much I remember. Two thousand-year-old water swirled below me, cloudy green round the piles, curving off downstream between low concrete pathways which looked scruffy and not much used, between trees and pale gold buildings that also looked as though they had been there since Rome began.

Crossing carefully at the lights, I was walking slowly now, partly because of the heat, partly because I wanted to prolong and relish this moment of discovery.

There, in that huge stadium ahead, in ten days, in my black and white New Zealand uniform, I'll march with four thousand other athletes.

And there, to the left, in the pool down there between two vast stands just coming into view, I'll swim in my black togs with the embroidered silver fern sewn on by Gran with her tiny even stitches. Twice, even if I don't get any further than the heats of my two events. I could see the trees around the pool now, as from the bus; the high diving platforms at the far end, the stands gradually opening up. Can you believe it, I was trembling. And then, shutting my eyes, with two last decisive steps to the railings . . .

. . . looking down onto the familiar shape of an Olympic-sized pool, people splashing in a clear blue, so dense it reminded me of Gran's blue-bag that she uses in the washing to make the whites whiter. Around it was a concourse of that dusky terracotta pink which even after only half a day in Rome I knew to be its special colour. Above both long sides towered these gigantic stands — ten times bigger than any pool at home. I saw them full of people and shivered. At the left-hand end was the separate diving pool, with the 10-metre tower that people braver than me throw themselves off. At the other end was a grassy slope with a huge black board where the results would be posted, (1st, A.B. Archer, New Zealand, dream on, Alex); underneath it a tunnel and behind it a red brick building with tall windows.

Behind the far stand rose the peak of a tree-covered hill which my map told me was the Monte Mario. I've seen lots of pools in my time: square, long, short, kidney-shaped, clean, scruffy, brand-new and very old; blue water, green, black, and all the shades in between; clear water, cloudy, murky, plain dirty, salt or fresh. This was as clear and sparkly as the world's bluest blue diamond, ringed by terracotta and dark green and without a doubt the most beautiful pool in the world.

It may sound strange, but I didn't go down immediately for that longed-for swim. I walked up and down the footpath enjoying the shade of the pines, the pleasure of the swimmers in the pool, lots of them children (not Swimmers, who only ever go up and down). According to my map, this was the Stadio del Nuoto, and the brick building next door was the Piscine Coni, with modern white pillars above an imposing set of steps. I followed a couple of brown-legged girls up, and found myself in a sort of lobby with bronze statues of naked men and glass walls looking down onto another pool: a smaller indoor one, the warm-up pool perhaps, with a spectacular mural of yet more naked men and horses up the far end and the left-hand wall of glass looking out over the Olympic pool.

No one really gave me more than a second glance as I sauntered back outside, but if I wanted a swim I had to find the entrance to the main pool, show my card, and find the changing-rooms. I realized I had no money.

ENTRATA was clear enough. I flashed my Games card

confidently, but the man inside the ticket office didn't seem inclined to let me in. 'Scusi, non capisco' I said when he finished talking. We looked at each other. Then, bolder, 'Desidero . . . ah . . .' and not knowing how to say 'a swim' I mimed the rest with my arms, breaststroke then freestyle. 'Per favore.'

'You are from New Zealand?' The man behind me wore the white shirt and look of an official. A short, square, sweaty Italian one who spoke English, but who wasn't all that friendly either.

'Yes. We've just arrived and I just want to have a swim.'

'There is special time for competitors. This is hour for the public.'

'I don't want to train. Just to have a swim please.'

'Competitors have special time.'

'I don't want special time, I just want to have a swim.'

'You are swimming competitor?'

'I'm an athlete.' It was true enough, as far as it went. Swimmers are athletes. I mightn't look much like a runner, but I could pass for a slimmer kind of shot-putter, or javelin thrower. He asked to see my identity card. I couldn't remember if it said what sport I was competing in. Apparently it didn't. 'Look, it's a hot day, I just want a swim.'

'New Zealand?'

'Si.'

'Beautiful country,' he said, examining my card minutely, as though he'd never seen one before or it might be forged.

'Si.' This was getting tedious, and making me cheeky. 'Molto bello.'

'Ah, parla italiano?'

'Non, I mean no and please can I go in for a swim? I'll pay, if that's the problem,' I said rashly. 'Per favore?' I said, holding out my hand for the card.

But somehow the little game had been played far enough. He looked at the man behind the counter and nodded. 'Thank you, grazie, molte grazie' I said, pulling my card from his pudgy fingers and scuttling through the turnstile before they changed their minds. These poolside buildings were concrete and tiles, and smelled of chlorine, just like all the others. I followed a girl through an archway marked DONNE and found myself in a large changing-room full of very brown people speaking Italian, loudly and very fast. For the first time in my life I felt bashful undressing, being a pale slug by comparison; however, I changed, put my top back on to cover what were obviously racing togs, and followed the same girl out to the pool.

The whole place was even more spectacular from the pool level. The stands looked vast, the surrounding pines and cypress trees black against the sky. I walked up onto the grass slope under the results board and spread myself in the sun, but my winter-white skin, already pink from the walk over, soon began to sizzle, and I had to move into the shade. I found myself dozing, half-dreaming of Andy, of lying with him in the sun at another Olympic pool over the other side of the world, lazily singing 'Summertime — and the livin' is easy', but without pain, just a gentle thankful sort of remembering.

Then I heard a loud announcement, not a word of which I understood, and the pool slowly began to clear. Public hour was over. The clock said 4.30. I couldn't dive in hurriedly; yet how long would it be before the competitors started to arrive and I could legitimately be here? Ah, Alex, how do you get yourself in these embarrassing situations?

I waited as long as I could. To my great relief, when there were only a few people left, a group of what were clearly Swimmers came out of the female changing-rooms, carrying the usual paraphernalia of towels and bags. It was obviously now Competitors' Time, so I slunk back into the empty changing-room, changed into another set of togs in the toilet, put on a bathing cap and strode out with a towel hiding my black bag, looking as though I owned the place.

Stupid, maybe, as if anyone would care really, but the last thing I wanted on my first day in Rome was long explanations involving Mr Upjohn and interpreters and an irate Italian official. Now, I had every right to be there.

At last, I had my swim. There were only four girls in the pool so far, churning away. The starting blocks looked higher above the water than at home, something I'd have to get used to. Anyone watching me probably thought I was just having a big languorous stretch or windmilling my arms the way swimmers do before they dive in, but it was actually a primitive and irresistible urge to lift up my arms to the trees and the sun and

9

say thank you, God and everyone else, for getting me here safely.

The water was bitingly cold on my overheated skin. I felt weightless, and, though I knew it wouldn't last long, utterly wonderful. The water felt every bit as good as it looked, like swimming in champagne.

Until I felt someone jab rudely at my shoulder as I turned. I looked up to see Mrs Churchill's round red and angry face leaning over me. I was not in her good books.

'Alex, I could put you over my knee, I could,' she panted. 'Have you no idea of the trouble you've caused? I searched the village, I woke up Zoe, I couldn't find Mr Upjohn . . .'

Thank goodness for that.

'I've run all the way over here, I couldn't get past the man at the ticket-office . . .' She sat down on the starting block, sweating heavily, fanning herself with her handbag. 'I know you were dying for a swim, but I have to say, I'm disappointed in you, going off by yourself without permission, without even telling me.'

'You were dead to the world,' I said.

'You should have woken me up if it was that urgent. I thought we agreed we'd all have a little rest first. Alex, you are NOT to go roaming round Rome by yourself ever again, is that clear? And no, I didn't tell Mr Upjohn.'

I hauled myself out of the pool, smiling at the pun, and gave her a sloppy fishy wet hug which I knew she didn't mind because she was so hot and because she was just as much relieved as angry.

'Thanks Mrs C for not telling. Clever Mrs C. Sorry Mrs C,' and she too couldn't help a twitch of a smile. It would certainly have been easier to have come here together, but a hundred times slower by the time she'd huffed and puffed her way from the village to the pool. And she'd have spoiled it, that first sight of the pool I'd worked so long and hard to compete in.

'You should come in, Mrs Churchill,' I said. 'It's *beautiful.*' I dived back in, did a dolphin dive or two, a pirouette, just for the sheer joy of it. Mrs Churchill was not pleased with me but she couldn't help herself smiling. 'It's *gorgeous.*' When I thought of that grubby dark pool I'd trained in twice a day for the past six months, the salt and badly treated water that left me nearly blind after each session . . . I did another set of twirls and swirls and dives. I was the dolphin I'd always known I once was or would be.

The changing-room was another whole new experience. When finally my five days in an aeroplane caught up with me and suddenly I couldn't swim another length, I found the changing-room now full of people arriving for their second training session of the day. I pretended to be preoccupied with dressing, but I was a new chum to this scene. There was lots of chat in several languages (two, Italian and French, I recognized — heaven knows what the others were). They wore smart track suits and skin-tight nylon togs in every colour under the sun, even white. Only black, dark green, and dull maroon had made it to the colonies so far, and my black togs looked pretty baggy and wrinkly and boring by comparison with these.

Along the benches were bags proclaiming U.S.A. Swim Team, South Africa, Italia, Canada, Sweden, something that looked like Hungary, Romania. No Brits or Aussies, thank heavens, the people most likely to say hello to a Kiwi. The Americans, whose striped togs were much the nicest, obviously all knew each other very well, and talked loudly among themselves about the price of hair sets in the village, going to see the Pope at St Peter's next Sunday, and having their bottoms pinched by randy Italians, taking absolutely no notice of anyone else.

Overall, though, behind the chat there was a brittle sort of tension. In ten days time we'd all be lining up against each other, the Americans against each other, too. In here, just as at home only more so, people would be watching what they said about their schedules, how they felt, which muscles were strained, which were hurting, when their periods were due, whether their time trials had been brilliant or lousy.

As I caught sight of myself in a mirror, I realized I was the only person in the entire dressing-area who was horribly, winterishly pale. Alongside the olive Italians and the golden California girls, my skin had an unhealthy bluish tinge, except on my shoulders where I'd caught some sun already. Compared with these healthy brown specimens, I didn't feel much of an international

11

athlete at all. I had an overwhelming urge to lie down on a soft bed and pass out.

But suddenly it hit me that there was something we did share — our size. Here, for the first time in my little life, despite my peculiar colour, I was normal. I was not the largest, tallest female in the room, the butch freak with the huge shoulders. This idea was so powerful that I sat down on the bench. I looked up at all these fantastic bodies in various stages of undress. We were birds of a feather. In countries where there were big swimming communities and lots of competition, these tall girls would train and race together and it probably didn't cross their minds; but there'd only ever been one of me, the 'big girl' — 'Juno-esque', a stupid reporter once called me — who'd always been so much taller than Maggie and the rest. Here five foot ten and a quarter was normal, just your common or garden female body. Normal, at last!

'You from Noo Zealand?'

I was caught off guard. The dark-haired girl next along the bench was pulling on a pair of red togs, and her bag said Canada. She sounded utterly amazed that anyone should come from Noo Zealand. 'Yes,' I said, bracing myself for another query about my bea-uuuu-tiful country or just how long was the bridge between Sydney and Auckland, which according to those who've travelled a lot is a standard question of friendly but very ignorant North Americans.

'Excuse me, but are you okay? You're so pale I thought . . .'

'I'm like this all the time. It's winter at home now.'

'That a fact? Do you get snow there?'

I had a great urge to say yes, Auckland was this very moment under ten feet of snow; but she was trying to be kind. She looked the sort of earnest type who might belong to a church choir. 'No, just rain, cold, gales, more rain.'

Was it obvious that I was suddenly feeling homesick, stomach-sick, tired-sick and on the verge of a second explosion of tears? As I stood up, the room started to swim. I sat down again, pretending to get something out of my bag, willing myself to stand and walk out of the dressing shed without the total embarrassment of falling over in a roomful of foreign-speaking strangers.

'When did you arrive? How many in your team?' she said as I fumbled with my things.

'Today and just me.'

'Just one? *One* swimmer!' Having just taken her glasses off, she peered down and examined me closely. 'Glory be! Poor you. By the way, I'm Barbara, I do backstroke.'

'I'm Alex, freestyle . . . um, excuse me . . . see you later . . .' Sorry, Barbara backstroker, if you thought I was unfriendly but . . . I made it to the door, steadied myself along the tiled corridor, launched out across the concourse to where Mrs Churchill was waiting to take me home, feeling very weak at the knees. I dared not even look at the pool which was now full of no doubt very famous people churning up and down breaking world records. The first day of school was over. Tomorrow I wouldn't be a new chum. The New Zealand swimming team asked her chaperone, very humbly, if they could possibly get a taxi back to the village.

Born on a thirteenth

'Go to Rome, young man,' said my teacher as we sat, an uneasy thirteen, at dinner three nights ago in Milan. Our number had been noted early in the evening; I alone welcomed it, for I was born on a thirteenth, and too many good and/or interesting things have happened to me on thirteenths to discount as coincidence.

Though I hadn't then been to Rome, I demurred. The city, I said, would be packed full of tourists and beautiful but brainless Olympic athletes. Ah, they all agreed, but consider, La Grande Olimpiade! Aspiring singers should know something about crowds and large audiences; particularly those who come from a country which has virtually no people in it at all! You'll understand something of Rome when you hear the crowds roar in the Stadio Olimpico, they said. Go to see *Aida* at the Terme di Caracalla, outdoors, in the moonlight, they said. *Aida!* I needed little more persuading.

Even better, it transpired that Enrico, one of the older students also at dinner, was driving down to Rome, taking two days, returning a car to an aunt, and then going with her on holiday to Scotland, of all places, somewhere cool, quiet, and raw. The upshot was a seat in a splendid 1947 Alfa Romeo to Rome, and an empty apartment to stay in when I got there.

My only duties would be twofold; to help get the pair of them out to the airport on Saturday morning, she being an elderly and nervous traveller who liked courtiers about her to carry bags; and to feed an equally ancient Pekingese dog called Turandot who has apparently never left the apartment, which is near the Terme di Caracalla, for fifteen years.

I write this, in that apartment, on a thirteenth (August 13),

15

beginning a new journal. My English, I suspect, skipping through eighteen months and nearly five hundred pages of my last journal, the chronicle of a Kiwi innocent abroad, has acquired a formality of tone which would raise eyebrows in the Land of the Long White Shroud; unless there has been a miraculous change since I left which actually encourages schoolboys and grown men to speak in sentences. To voice an opinion on something, anything, other than rugby and race horses.

This apartment is the epitome of cool Roman elegance, huge and sparsely furnished (cf a New Zealand house of wood with its china cabinets and colonial clutter), yet I don't feel lonely, just very privileged, surrounded by paintings, furnishings and porcelain of restrained beauty. Enrico's ancient aunt turned out to be less ancient than he pictured, but tall and patrician, not unlike a Roman version of Virginia Woolf, and not long retired as principal flautist with one of the Rome orchestras.

I received my standing orders for the dog Turandot, which resembles a bedraggled sheepskin slipper, and was given a brass key large enough to lock up the Victor Emmanuel II memorial. We left the apartment in a cloud of deep gloom — the fates had decreed that she would not, of course, return from this holiday. She hoped that the plane would at least honour her immortal soul and crash on Italian heads, not the chilly Swiss, the unmusical English, or worse still, the French. Her other nephew Ruggiero knew the bank where her will was kept. He would settle her affairs, as she was laid to rest in a common foreign grave. Enrico, a tenor, was becoming more than slightly hysterical.

As chauffeur for the day, I stylishly drove the Alfa Romeo to the airport and back, to stable it permanently in the garage below. Mercifully, from what I experienced of Roman traffic today, the car does not go with the apartment. By the time I put both my passengers on the plane, I was wondering if all our stars were foretelling disaster.

Except — this is a thirteenth. Reluctant to tackle the traffic until I'd had a beer and studied a street map, I wandered over to the arrivals lounge, reminded, by all the flags and music, that this is Rome in festive mood, that the Olympics start in about ten days. Perhaps I might see some of the teams arrive, a film star, a head of state. I can spend hours people-watching, and I am on holiday.

Curiously, or perhaps not for a thirteenth, it was during that hour that I saw the New Zealand team emerge from Customs — the largest, indeed the only group of Kiwis I have seen since my departure. If they'd come direct, it wasn't surprising they looked so travel-worn, trailing shoulder bags and black blazers, with the dazed eyes of a bunch of idiotic herded sheep. There were about forty men, at a guess; mostly smaller physically than I would have imagined, probably athletes and hockey players, about my height; older men who were obviously officials; short but brawny types who must have been weightlifters and boxers, with pugnacious noses and tight shirts; a couple of giants.

The six or seven women were in better shape. One was much younger than the others, and stood apart. Very tall, very slim but broad in the shoulder, long arms, maybe seventeen or eighteen. Very short hair, but she wore the drab uniform with a certain grace, more than the rest of them put together; also utterly and defiantly miserable. A distance runner, javelin thrower maybe? A swimmer?

As I watched, a well-dressed man, one of the welcoming party, went across and spoke to her. He was solicitous, but whatever was said looked like bad news; he led her crying to a seat. Unlike most girls, she wept openly, not trying to conceal her need. Something from home, a death, an accident, a reason to turn around and fly straight back? But after one of the officials joined them, I wasn't so sure. As she recovered from the tears, her face cleared like a flower opening after rain. Everything about her sang, vibrated with life. She looked as though a great weight had been lifted off those superb shoulders.

I went out of the swing doors. I could pass for an Italian bystander, of which there are always plenty. Behind my dark glasses, I saw the team straggle out to the bus, heard snatches of English: Cripes it's hot, complaints about swollen legs and entreaties to the manager to stop for a beer. I had forgotten how strong the Kiwi accent is, how raw the vernacular. I had no desire to speak to them, to identify myself as a countryman, even to wish them luck.

17

The girl came among the last. Closer she was, as were they all coming from a New Zealand winter, extremely pale, with dark rings under her eyes, but somehow triumphant too. She looked straight through me, clearly not a girl who smiles at strange men, but her eyes were warm, a curious grey-blue; indeed her whole face was curious, strong, not pretty, with wide-set eyes under a pair of straight eyebrows that owed nothing to the current fashion for plucking, and splendid bone structure. Not a typical New Zealand face, if there is such a thing; for a girl, too direct, too calculating. The rest of the team looked only barely alive, but she actually bounced up the steps. I watched her move down the bus, find an inside seat. Even from there, I could feel the force of her personality as she talked with the older woman next to the window. A chaperone, probably.

I had not intended to make contact with the team. Two or three Italian contacts, maybe, none very compelling; I may follow up the offer of a Vespa motor scooter. I have a week to see Rome, and then a few extra days to see some of the Games events if I can get tickets. Perhaps the opening ceremony, some of the athletics, the fencing, gymnastics, the swimming. Maybe she is a swimmer. I don't intend to make contact.

Staking out the territory

That first night I went to bed while it was still daylight and Zoe and all the others were having dinner. I slept for thirteen hours. No 5.30 alarm, no nightmares of Andy drowning, car accidents, swimming in glue or making a fool of myself on a stage; my first total zonked-out sleep for two years. Mrs Churchill got all peculiar about the idea of me missing dinner, but the very thought of food and another roomful of strangers made me feel ill.

Besides, I had this new and heady sensation of lightness. No one here knew anything about me or my times or the fact that I'd never swum in an international race in my life. No one expected me to win a medal or even get into the final. Back home, they knew I was up against Dawn Fraser and the American wonderkids and they just wanted me to do my best. I went off to sleep naked under a sheet, light-headed and smiling.

I'll never know if the bells were real. Did I dream them, the bells ringing at dawn, the magical beginning of the third act of *Tosca* when the shepherd boy sings to his sheep? I listened to the record at home often enough. Or did I really hear the distant bells of the city, St Peter's and the rest, all on different notes, calling? Real or dreamed, no matter, I slid blissfully back to sleep, hearing bells.

'Alex? Are you alive? Wake up.'

Behind my eyelids I registered light, warmth, sweet female smells, my own hot smell. Voices outside, not English, traffic, car horns. Where on earth was I?

'Alex!' An older voice, worried. A weight sat on my bed. Someone had hold of my toe. *'Alex?'*

19

I'd become paralysed in the night, I'd picked up polio in Calcutta, I was about to be carted off to an iron lung.

I prised a sticky eyelid half open, and saw a prim lady with fuzzy grey hair and glasses, wearing a white embroidered blouse of the sort bought in Singapore. Mrs . . . Churchill, ah, *right*, my chaperone and I'm in Rome for the Olympics.

'How do you feel?'

I'm in Rome to swim in the Olympics!

'How do you feel, Alex?'

'She's okay, Mrs Churchill. Look at her grinning.' That must be Zoe, my high-jumping room-mate, sounding quite chirpy.

'It's breakfast time, Alex. You must have some food.'

'What's the time?'

'Nearly eight. You've been asleep for thirteen hours.'

'Mmmmmmmmm.' No cat ever had such a stretch. Did I dream that beautiful pool surrounded with pine trees, the turquoise water? No, I didn't. For the first time in months, despite a low-down gut-ache, I couldn't wait to go training.

'You were out cold last night,' said Zoe, brushing her long hair. 'You just died. I've never seen anyone drop off so quickly.'

'Were you here?'

'Don't you remember?'

'No.' I must have sleepwalked too. At the pool, with me upright, but only just, we'd got a taxi after some lengthy pidgin English-Italian chat and a long wait. There'd been a small problem with Italian money, because neither of us had any. I had to grovel to borrow some temporarily from an official at the village, while Mrs C stayed with the upset taxi driver. I think.

'What day of the week is it?'

'Sunday.'

'Can we go to St Peter's?'

'Tiger for punishment, you are,' said Mrs Churchill, shuffling a folio full of papers. 'You've got training and we'll talk about it over breakfast. I remember reading . . . yes, there's a special audience next Sunday for all the Olympic athletes.'

Next Sunday! It seemed a year away. My side of the room looked like a bomb went off. It had looked pretty bare yesterday when we walked in, like a school hostel. There were no pictures on the pink walls, and the furniture was mostly built-in, with a big mirror above the dressing-table. Zoe, one of those tidy types, had already got herself organized into drawers and taken up more than half the dressing-table space with her bottles and junk.

During the night something else had also happened. As I began to get out of bed, I felt, smelt, and saw that my first period in over six months had well and truly arrived, explaining the gut-ache. 'Shit.'

'Alex!'

'Oh hell.' I pulled the sheet back quickly and leant over to pull my dressing-gown from my exploded bag. Thank God Mum the nurse hadn't listened to me when I did my packing. I'd shouted at her *I'm not going to have a period ever again,* but she'd insisted that I bring the proper equipment.

'What's the matter?' asked Mrs Churchill.

'Cramp, I think or . . .' I wobbled my calf muscle from side to side, and flexed my foot up and down convincingly. 'Might have pulled something.' Five minutes later Mrs C had satisfied herself that I didn't need Mr Upjohn to find a physio immediately, I wasn't out of the Games, and I probably would walk again. Eventually I persuaded her and Zoe to go on over to breakfast, after she'd given me detailed instructions on how to get to our dining hall.

Despite the mess, I was pleased that my new slim body — my clothes told me I'd lost a few more pounds on the journey over — was in working order again. It's a bit odd, when you're nearly sixteen and as virginal as it's possible to be, to go without a period for over six months. Stress, Mum had said flatly, but I knew she'd worried about it.

It took me a while to clean everything up. Along with myself I washed the sheets in the shower. I hung them in the wardrobe, and scrubbed at the blood on the mattress with my face flannel and plenty of cold water. Most of it came out. It would dry quickly, in this heat. *Very* embarrassing, but . . . at least my period would be well over by my first race. My body was obviously telling me something.

Even at 8.30 in the morning the sun was fierce, and rock 'n roll music was blaring out across the brown grass. There were lots more people strolling round in track suits than yesterday. Mostly men, I noted, keeping well away from anyone. You could walk underneath the brown buildings — they were built on these funny legs. Everything, buildings, trees, grass, looked dusty and dry and brand-new, only just finished off in time.

I found our dining hall easily. It was bigger than a school hall and about as plain, and seemed to be for us Kiwis and two or three other teams. Mrs Churchill waved at me from one end of a long table full of our men in black track suits, tucking into breakfast. Zoe had found her athletic mates. I walked over, my gut-ache worse, remembering just in time to limp slightly.

'Morning, Alex,' a few voices cried, waving breadrolls or forkfuls of sausage. 'How's your leg?' asked Mrs Churchill, looking anxious.

'Not too bad. Where's Mr Upjohn?' I said, before she could go on about it.

'Probably still asleep. He had a managers' meeting last night.'

'Ah,' I said cynically. I'd heard about managers' meetings, with a few drinks.

'Alex, he was very tired,' she said indignantly, but she knew what I meant.

'Of course he was.'

She grinned. 'Go and get some food, dear.' I looked at her plateful of goodies and suddenly realized I was *ravenously* hungry.

I had never seen such food. To get the cooked part of the breakfast you had to queue army-style in front of a long serving area manned by middle-aged Italians acting as pantomime cooks, in white tunics like dentists and tall picture-book baker's hats. But they knew about food — there were nutty cereals and fresh fruits, huge jugs of juices, cooked eggs and bacon and tomatoes and meat and sausages, breads and sweet rolls and jams and coffees, laid out like a banquet. '*Wow*,' I said, and a tall brown man in front turned and grinned. He had the blackest, tightest hair I'd ever seen.

'Who are these people?' I said as I unloaded my tray of some oaty/nutty mixture called muesli, fruit, bacon and eggs, bread roll, and coffee.

'The very dark handsome ones are Moroccans,' said Mrs C.

'The handsome white ones in the green track suits are South Africans.'

Interesting! Someone in this village was either ignorant or had a sense of humour. Even I knew that our All Blacks and their Springboks were currently slogging it out in South Africa; you couldn't avoid knowing, front page stuff every day at home, all about a few games of rugby. One win each, including a very strange game in Cape Town with the crowd of Coloureds cheering for the All Blacks, not for their own country. A draw yesterday and the deciding Test in two weeks.

I tried my muesli. It was a bit floury, but chewy, and good too. I wondered, as I chewed, if the fair-haired South Africans over there knew about the protests in New Zealand. I'd walked with Keith Jameson and two thousand other people up Queen Street, on a march organized to protest against the team going to South Africa without Maori players to keep the South Africans happy. For my pains I got my cheesecake picture on the front page of the paper and an official reprimand. That was three months ago. The team still went.

Even here we couldn't get away from the damn game. 'Yeah, okay, a draw, but the Springbok pack's bloody walking all over us,' I heard from the table behind me. I looked around, and saw a group of our men hobnobbing with a group of South Africans, and guess what they were talking about!

'Damn,' I said. 'They'll talk about nothing else all next week but bloody rugby. Or fight about it.'

'Alex, dear,' Mrs C chided me, yet again.

'The All Blacks should never have gone.'

'Not here, please. It's a dead issue.'

Light blue touch-paper, retire. 'Tell that to the Maori players who got left behind because their skin's brown.' The two hockey players opposite glanced up from their plates, surprised.

'They said, no Maori players were good enough to go.'

'Convenient. It's the principle, don't you see?'

'I see people round us, different colours and different races, all talking, all here for one thing, the Olympics,' she said firmly. 'We'll have no more talk of rugby.'

'Suits me, Mrs C,' I said.

'Much more to the point — we've got ten days to get you fit.'

23

Right on cue, Mr Upjohn appeared with his tray loaded up with cooked goodies and bread rolls, like there'd never be a lunch. 'Morning Alex, and how are we today?'

'Fine,' I lied, because since I began to eat my gut-ache had got considerably worse. He didn't look too good himself, but then track suits don't look all that good on older people with barrel chests, big bottoms, wet hair from showering, and a hangover. He'd also cut himself shaving.

'She's got a leg problem, maybe a pulled calf muscle,' said Mrs Churchill.

'No, it's okay, really,' I said hastily.

'Should we ask to see a doctor?' said Mr Upjohn.

'No truly, it's not that bad. It might have been cramp. I was half asleep.'

'Well, keep me posted, Alex.' He attacked his fruit with enthusiasm. 'I hear the third Test at Bloemfontein was a great game.' I grinned *I told you so* at Mrs Churchill. 'That's one each,' he said chewing away, 'and a draw. What a game the fourth Test will be! An absolute classic!'

The man was in Rome for the Olympics, thanks to me, and now he wishes he was in South Africa watching rugby! There was no pleasing some people.

'It's not a proper New Zealand team. I won't spill any tears if the Springboks win. We shouldn't have been there in the first place, and it's a rough and disgusting game anyway,' I said riskily and apparently loudly, because now a number of surprised faces along both sides of the table were looking at me.

'Alex, you really must . . .'

'Hear, hear,' said the hockey player opposite, a skinny chap with thin gingery hair. Well, support from a hockey player would figure. Andy once told me that rugby players think that anyone who plays hockey is a poof. Actually I think it's a much more intelligent and skilful game than rugby. He raised his coffee cup in a sort of toast. 'I was in that march up Queen Street too. That picture of you in the paper . . .'

'. . . was very embarrassing,' I said quickly, because Mr Upjohn had written me a snotty letter complaining about it, threatening that I might find myself withdrawn from the Rome team if I continued to get involved in controversial issues like protest marches. I couldn't resist adding, 'I think it was rigged.'

Mr Upjohn glanced up, then at Mrs Churchill, while the hockey player looked interested, but was tactful enough not to pursue the subject. There was a long silence while we all concentrated on digging out our melons and munching on our muesli, which I have to admit was much more interesting than Weet-Bix. The pain in my gut had gone from bad to worse. I'd rather lost my enthusiasm for beginning training today.

'Now, dear,' said Mrs Churchill finally, doing what women always do when they're feeling uncomfortable, i.e. rummaging around in her handbag. 'Now let's talk about today. Where's that list of training times?'

'I'd rather rest today. Or go to St Peter's or somewhere.'

Mr Upjohn got on his coach's look. 'Your first swim, Alex; don't you think, after that long rest yesterday, you should be getting to grips with your schedule?'

Conspirator Mrs Churchill put her head down and started to rummage in her papers again.

'I've got my period, Mr Upjohn. It came last night. Actually it's the first for six months and rather heavy and giving me a gut-ache.'

'Alex *dear*,' said Mrs Churchill, so embarrassed she didn't know where to look. Girls don't talk about periods in mixed company, particularly at breakfast in front of strange hockey players. Why not? He was wearing a wedding ring and presumably knew about these things? Mr Upjohn had grown-up daughters and grandchildren too. Why shouldn't men know about something which happened to females twelve moontimes a year for most of their lives? And Mrs C, you're the worst, because you were more concerned about the men being embarrassed than you were with my gut-ache and what you could do about it. I flashed them all a brilliant and unrepentant smile.

'I'd like to just . . . well, go for a long walk, by the river. Walk round the village, look at the stadium. Tomorrow I'll start, promise.'

She tried to hide it, but her face dropped at the prospect of a long walk with me. She sighed. Duty called. 'Over to you, Enid,'

25

said Mr Upjohn, very embarrassed, also relieved it wasn't him who had to put on his walking shoes. He pushed his half-eaten plate of bacon and eggs away. I think I might have put him off his breakfast.

Actually, wanting to go for a long walk was for a more primitive reason than simply keeping out of the pool with a very heavy period. I'd always trained, raced, whatever through periods, no problem. Some girls had old-fashioned mothers who thought it was bad for them and unhygienic, but I think that's old wives' tales; it's not cupfuls of blood, only teaspoons, if that, and cold water stops it, and anyway, think of all those small boys peeing in public pools, I bet!

I could have fixed the gut-ache with a codeine, and ignored the heavy bloated feeling. After all those days sitting in aeroplanes, I just wanted to stake out the territory, walk on the warm earth, smell the trees, absorb the sun through my skin, work out where everything was, so I knew where I was.

Begin to feel — because I don't feel it yet — like an athlete whose whole life has been working towards being here, a competitor at La Grande Olimpiade.

Mrs Churchill, who Zoe had dubbed the Bulldog, wasn't a bad old stick to spend a day with. We changed some money at the Banco di Roma and bought stamps at the Ufficio Postale. To my astonishment, there was a letter for me! From Mum, saying how proud she was, they all were, how she just *knew* (written well before I left, when things were looking pretty grim for both Maggie and me) that things would be all right. She loves me. More than enough to bring tears to my eyes. There was also a 'Welcome to Rome' telegram from darling Mr Jack which had the same effect. We bought postcards and writing paper from the souvenir shop; we couldn't *believe* the prices posted outside the beauty salon and Bulldog decided she might shout herself just one hair-set while she's here, and I decided I'll stick with my wisps.

We walked through the recreation areas where athletes, black, white, and every colour in between, were lounging around formica tables drinking Coke, keeping the juke-box going. I persuaded Bulldog we should have a Coke and one song, a new Elvis Presley 'It's Now or Never', which I thought pretty soppy and Bulldog couldn't *stand.* Then we wandered out through the main gates. We decided we knew only seven of the dozens of flags flying above the gates, and headed across the bridge towards the stadium. It was already too hot for walking, but we're stubborn Kiwis who don't mind a bit of sun and we wanted to see the stadium.

Empty theatres have always fascinated me, school halls, pools, wherever you get performers and audiences. They're full of memories, ghosts, music, people laughing and crying, if only you stand for a while and listen. This stadium was different. We found an entrance, showed our identity cards to an attendant who spoke English and understood that we just wanted to have a look. He showed us through a corridor, up some steps, and pointed us towards the sunlight.

I know I gasped. I'd imagined *nothing* like this. We were surrounded by stands, four tiers high, with groups of flagpoles around the rim. In front of us was a grassy football field, dwarfed by the red running track and another circle of grass. A gigantic scoreboard loomed over one end. We turned around slowly, speechless. It was brand new; there were no ghosts, no music here yet, but it was waiting. 'Blimey Charlie!' Bulldog said finally. 'And we think Eden Park is the centre of the universe!'

That wasn't all. We were even more overcome when we wandered into the smaller stadium next door, through the red brick buildings next to the Piscine Coni I had discovered yesterday. White paved courtyards led us on through an avenue of white twice-life-size male bodies, carrying cloaks, wearing sandals, with veins in their marble legs and rib bones showing through, and figleafs on the skimpy side. I think it was a bit much for Bulldog. In the stadium itself, a whole circle of huge statues stood white against the trees behind and looked down on a low oval of marble seats and a terracotta running track. We hadn't expected this. We found out later it was the 'severe Greek-styled' Stadio dei Marmi. It was my classical history books come alive. Children were training on the track. On the grassy square in the middle they were practising long jumps, throwing the discus, javelins. If I imagined them naked and glistening with oil, I was back in ancient Greece. It wasn't a film set, it was for real, a real living classical Greek stadium here and now, a beautiful space for beautiful free bodies.

I stood there like a stunned mullet and thought, what *else* was there for me to discover, jewels like this which weren't even in the guidebooks? I knew about the Colosseum, but what else? Below us five boys, about fourteen-year-olds, lined up for a race, dancing around as runners do. I could feel my own limbs twitching, longing to be back in my element, which is water. I could forget the throbbing ache in my lower tum. I was beginning, just beginning, to feel like an athlete again.

By lunch time we were both wilting badly, and decided to walk back along the road above the river. If I'd thought breakfast was amazing, lunch was out of this world: unknown vegetables and fruits in salads, olive oil and wine vinegar that you pour on separately, great trays of red-flecked salamis, pizzas dripping with mushrooms and stringy pale cheese, meats with green-flecked stuffings, something called pistachio, purple figs and apricots, rich cakes dusted with icing sugar, cut into small pieces, not like Gran's hunks of orange sponge-cake squelching cream. We had three weeks of this! Now I knew why they had siestas in Italy, and it wasn't just the heat.

When I woke my gut-ache was gone. It was after five. I thought of the statues around that elegant Greek stadium, the inviting blue of the pool, and shivered with excitement.

Now it was time to get out my folio of programmes, papers. Tho' it was all in Italian, the swimming programme was clear enough, with the events and competitors' names after the usual pictures of the chairmen of this and that committee.

Venerdì, 25 agosto, the swimming starts. Famous names leapt out at me: Dawn Fraser and Lorraine Crapp, Ilsa Konrads, Jon Konrads, Murray Rose, John Devitt — Australians all. Dawn Fraser's main rival Chris Von Saltza and the fourteen-year-old wunderkind Carolyn Wood, both U.S.A., a few famous Dutch and British names I knew — what the hell was I doing there? A little foreign fish of very ordinary species about to get chewed up and spat out by all the famous sharks.

There was my name, Sig. Alexandra B. Archer (N.Z.), in the fifth and last Batteria of the women's 100m Stile Libero, 15.00 to

16.00, which probably meant 3 to 4 in the afternoon. Not good for me, that was my sleepy time, my lowest ebb. I'd have to adjust my body-clock in the week to come — somehow push all my routine forwards or backwards so that I could be wide awake, up and running ready to hit the water around 3.45 p.m.

The Semi-finale, sixteen fastest times, *if* I made it that far, were on the following day, 20.40 to 21.20. Night-time — better.

The Finale, eight fastest times, why was I bothering, the *Finale* was on Monday, August 29, at 21.00 - 21.20, best time for me 'cause I'd always been a night person. Ha ha, Alex — you in the final, don't be bloody silly. You're off your rocker. Oh yes? The 400 metre Stile Libero, not really my event, had heats on Wednesday 31, at night. The Finale was the following night. Well, at worst I'd swim twice in the Rome Olympics.

I was dreaming impossible dreams when Zoe bounced in, full of the great training facilities in the village, trampolines and the like, and meeting the Aussies and Canadians she got to know at the last Empire Games in Cardiff. She'd made arrangements for sightseeing, restaurants, the lot. Bully for her.

After dinner, another banquet listening to our team men swopping training experiences, Bulldog and I went for a short stroll round the village in the pink twilight. It was obviously a custom, tho' Bulldog told me that half the teams, especially from other European countries, hadn't even arrived yet.

In the recreation areas the juke-box was going flat out, 'Let's Twist Again Like We Did Last Summer', and a few couples in American track suits showed me what the Twist looked like. I watched my first television but the novelty soon wore off 'cause there's a limit to how long you can watch an oldish man gabbling away in Italian. The main events of the Games were to be televised, but I didn't suppose I'd see any 'cause I'd be *there*. I'd have to wait for the film later. I saw a few of our men walking around, easily spotted in our black track suits. They were friendly enough, said hello, howyadoing lass, alright? but by the time I went up the stairs for my second night in my pink bed I wondered how I was going to last five more *weeks* of feeling younger and lonelier than anyone in the village, in Rome, in the universe.

Only five days away from home, and I never thought I'd feel such an aching hungry need to talk to someone the same age as me, from the same country . . . who talked the same language . . .

A letter from a friend

It was undoubtedly a most strange coincidence that I should have been at the airport yesterday when the team arrived. They reminded me of much I've left behind: the dour quasi-English manner, the plain creased shirts, the baggy grey trousers and appalling short-back-and-sides haircuts I also once wore; indeed that women should form so insignificant a part of a national sports team. Altogether, they looked more like a third-grade brass band hurriedly outfitted at the local branch of Farmers and sent off to a world convention in Kentucky, than the world-class athletes they supposedly are.

Equally strange was this morning, while unpacking, finding the letter I had received the day we left Milan and had tossed unopened into my bag. I get little mail from New Zealand these days. My uncle wrote once before his stroke, a last plea to come to my senses; aunt, rarely, my cousins, never. Last Christmas, some cards from my old piano teacher, from varsity friends keeping me up with gossip and earth-shattering events like the bridge opening in Auckland and television starting this year. They made the ludicrous assumption that, with the Games in Italy, I'd naturally be in Rome to cheer my countrymen on.

Against my own inclinations, nevertheless, I am here. I wouldn't have known who was in the team, nor their chances of success, nor even remembered seeing them at the airport, had it not been for the letter I opened this morning.

It came from a teacher in Auckland, a woman called Marcia Macrae, reminding me that she met me two years ago after a University Drama Club performance of *Julius Caesar* in which I played (against my physical type) a deviously smooth and menacing Cassius. My name had intrigued her. Afterwards we

31

established that I was indeed the bastard son of her pre-war drama school friend from New Zealand. She'd been devastated by my mother's death.

Having since heard that I was studying in Italy, she was writing simply to say that a pupil of hers, Alexandra Archer, from Auckland, was shortly to be in Rome with the New Zealand Olympic Games team. (The letter, from the postmark, had taken full twelve days to get here.) She was the only swimmer in the team — the other chosen swimmer, Alex's close rival, having sadly been struck down with peritonitis just before the team left.

If I happened to be in Rome during the Games, we might meet. Alex would, she knew, be very appreciative, would enjoy meeting someone who knew Italy. As for her chances in the Games, Marcia knew little about swimming, but Alex was an unusual young woman; she would not be the slightest bit surprised if she burst on the world sporting scene like a firework. As for the rest, the local papers were predicting that Murray Halberg, the distance runner, was about the best and only prospect for a medal.

Today, Sunday August 14, I have luxuriated in a morning spent sleeping late, investigating the apartment's large collection of long-playing records and the considerable virtues of the German baby grand; also some practice, a pleasure in this high-ceilinged resonant room. My practice disturbed Turandot not one iota. She spends most of her time curled up in a basket, asleep. Wearing my newest straw hat, I went for a walk to find a local trattoria for a late lunch, enjoying my anonymity and the familiarity of waiters who no longer pick me immediately as a foreigner but (I think) accept me as Italian-speaking, Italian-dressed, Italian-born; from the accent, Milano, somewhere in Lombardy. After just eighteen months here, that's progress. I must see how long I can keep this up.

A firework? That would fit the burning grey eyes, the buoyant step into the bus of the tall girl I saw at the airport yesterday. Alexandra Archer, pupil of someone who knew my unknown and unlamented mother. I have to admit to a slight resentment; these are the very obligations I left home to avoid and forget.

I have spent the whole evening, this first Sunday in Rome,

32

listening to a new recording of *Aida.* Zinka Milanov and Jussi Bjoerling, utterly marvellous. Tomorrow I must get a ticket for the production under the moonlight.

Strange, if I hadn't found that letter, I would probably have forgotten the luminous fine-boned girl in the white shirt and grey skirt.

Let it here be recorded, I have tonight been listening to *Aida* and I have not thought about Alexandra Archer at all.

A hot and dangerous place

'Sorry Alex, no training this morning,' said Mr Upjohn flatly, unloading his repulsive breakfast tray across the table. 'You've got another obligation.'

Between mouthfuls of muesli and melon, I'd been going through the programme with Bulldog, explaining about adjusting my body-clock to be fighting fit at 3.45 p.m. on *venerdì ventisei agosto*. My training sessions were at 9.30 each day, along with the Aussies, Brits, Canadians, and some European teams.

I'd vaguely registered that some of our men seemed to be rather well-dressed for breakfast, in uniform trousers and shirts and carrying blazers, but Mr Upjohn was actually wearing his, *and* had put brylcreme on his hair. What obligation? I was starting training this morning.

'Our flag-raising ceremony is at ten, in the main compound.' he said.

'Do I have to go?'

'Naturally,' he said, shocked. 'The whole team goes. It's our first time, marching together as a team. The press will be there. Reporting time is 9.30.'

'I wasn't told about this,' said Bulldog.

'I'm telling you now.'

'It's a little late, isn't it?'

Mr Upjohn munched his breadroll, said good morning to several of the other managers, heartily. Bulldog looked at me, obviously very annoyed, warning me against saying anything rash. 'Eat up, Alex,' she said. 'We'll have to go back and change.'

We made it back in time, togged out in blazers, white high heels and all, but only just. Zoe had been out training and

35

forgotten her watch and had to climb into her uniform all flushed and sweaty. Out in the main compound ringed by flagpoles, the managers put us in lines, four abreast, the officials first, then us six women, then all the men. We marched in like an army, left right, another novelty for me. I was still thinking this was a waste of good training time, and sweltering in my black wool blazer, but there's something about a flag when you're a long way from home. Our flag with the four stars of the Southern Cross was slowly raised while the small band played 'God Defend New Zealand' (badly, the trumpets flat, sounded as though they were sight-reading it). No one actually sang. I was too choked up to sing, mighty patriotic and homesick all at once.

After that, we stood while the band trumpeted up the Japanese, Ethiopian, and Chilean flags too, their teams likewise ninety per cent male. Afterwards we could only shake hands and grin stupidly at each other. They didn't speak a word of English, nor us a word of Japanese or Spanish or whatever it is Ethiopians speak. Various people tried speaking pidgin English very loudly and distinctly, as though to idiots. It didn't work. We bowed and scraped. The Japanese nodded like dolls, the Chileans grinned, and the Ethiopians looked solemn.

Then I heard a female voice close by: 'Shake a Japanese hand? Never.' Bulldog joined Zoe and me, rummaging in her handbag. 'Don't ask me. Never!' she muttered, looking extremely flushed and unhappy. Behind us a group of our officials with two blank-faced Japanese bowed carefully at each other. The Japanese went to join their team. One of our officials came over to us, loosening his tie. 'Enid, that was inexcusable.' 'I'm sorry,' she said, 'but I will never . . .' 'For Chrissake, Enid, you must, it's fifteen years . . .' Behind her hanky she said, 'My husband, aged twenty-four, died in Burma at the hands of those people and you tell me I *must?*' Zoe and I were looking at each other. 'This is no place for politics, harbouring grudges,' he said, mopping his forehead. Hadn't she said the same to me about the South Africans? 'No, then what about Hitler's games in Berlin and that water-polo match between Hungary and Russia, drawing blood, only four years ago?' she shot back, surprising me. 'We fought the Italians too,' he said, 'and I was one of them, in the Western

Desert, at El Alamein, liberating Rome. According to your . . .'
'The Japs were different,' she said defensively. 'I'm sorry, I know it's not logical . . . I'll avoid them, we don't get Japs in Christchurch, not in Riccarton, but don't you tell me I must . . .'

On the verge of tears, she looked at me. 'I can't expect you to understand, Alex, you were just a baby.' I didn't understand. My Dad came home from the war; lots didn't, from Egypt, France, Crete, Singapore, Burma, all the other places I'd heard over the years. Italy too, so what should I be feeling about the Italians? I looked at the small backs of the Japanese team and wondered how they felt under all these cheerful flags; confused, angry, helpless, like me?

I'd noticed a few press people standing round, no one from home I recognized. We were interrupted by a lanky British reporter, the *Daily Mail* on duty in immaculate white shirt, club tie, crinkly hair, big sunburnt nose, panama hat. What did it feel like, ladies, to be the team that had travelled the longest distance to get here? 'Sick of aeroplanes,' said Zoe distantly. Were we homesick? 'No,' I said. Had we left behind boyfriends? I thought a British reporter might have asked more sensible questions. Zoe mumbled something about her fiancé in Wellington.

And what did we Kiwis think of the All Blacks' chances for the all-important fourth Test in South Africa? I was about to say who cared, when Bulldog coughed very loudly; so I told him I'd be glued to the BBC live broadcast even if it cost me sleep or training time, and absolutely *devastated* if they let the country down. Don Clarke was my absolute hero, my pin-up boy, not forgetting Whineray and Pinetree Meads (I knew a few names because how can you not, when they're plastered all over our papers?) The national pride of the entire country was at stake. I watched rugby every Saturday, didn't everyone, the sheilas too, Ranfurly Shield, club matches, whatever; and by now, tho' the *Daily Mail* was lapping it up, the group had got bigger and several of our guys were beginning to look at me rather strangely; Zoe was trying to keep a straight face and Bulldog was desperate to stop me, which she did eventually by pretending to see Mr Upjohn in the crowd behind the *Daily Mail*. 'Oh yes, coming . . . you'll be late for training,' she cried. 'Excuse us, Alex has to . . . I'm sorry, but she simply must . . .' leading me off by the elbow.

'Oh you scamp! You absolute scamp! You know how that will get back home, I can just see it, Olympic swimmer Alex Archer is the All Blacks' greatest fan, she sleeps under a picture of Don Clarke. I never heard such *nonsense.*'

'No one cares what I think, Mrs C. Stupid questions get stupid answers. He wasn't interested, you see.'

Wrong again, Alex. It did get back home, in an N.Z.P.A./ Reuters round-up from Rome: *Rugby rivals share Olympic dining hall; South African and Kiwi athletes are shaping up over meals in the Olympic village for the final showdown between their rugby teams. Water-baby Alex Archer admits that 'The Boot' Don Clarke is her hero, will be among those listening to the live broadcast and cheering on their countrymen.* I didn't see the actual piece until someone sent the cutting in a letter, but I knew something must have appeared because I got a terse telegram from my university friend Keith Jameson who took me on the protest march three months ago.

TRAITOR, it said. YOUR FORMER MATE KEITH JAMESON. I went to the post office and fired back one of my own A JOKE THAT MISFIRED MI SCUSI MI DISPIACE CIAO and signed it LA BAMBINA DELL'ACQUA, much to the amusement of the post office clerk. But even that was communication of a sort. I stood in the Ufficio Postale and thought, I must be getting desperate if even the gnomish boorish randy hard-drinking fast-driving but somehow not entirely horrible Keith would be a welcome friend here. In all my swimming trips away from home, I'd never once been homesick. That was for miseryguts who didn't know when they were well off.

Never again would I be rude about people being homesick.

We got to the pool in time for a shortened training session. Mr Upjohn had discovered there were shuttle buses laid on. I took one look at the pool and thought: this is where it begins in earnest. The Aussies were the most obvious in their green and gold togs, brown as berries, swaggering and confident. I knew they'd all been to a training camp in Queensland. The world's top swim team no less, here to defend themselves against the strong U.S. team. I wasted a good ten minutes just sitting with Mrs C on the stands under her baby-blue umbrella, changed and ready to go, but turned to stone. For quite a while neither of us said a word.

This was the Olympics for real: about fifty world-class swimmers (and that wasn't even half of them) going like the clappers, churning up and down the blue water. No one looked tired; they all looked so horribly *fit*. Lots of officials, coaches with stopwatches, a few photographers getting action shots of Dawn Fraser training with two of the men, Lorraine Crapp, the famous Konrads Jon and Ilsa, Murray Rose; I recognized them all from photos but there were unknown younger Aussies, and Canadians in their red togs, and Brits with Union Jacks on theirs, who all looked just as fast and strong. No one looked younger than twenty. All the women looked like Amazons, but it was the men who knocked me out, because most of the 'men' swimming in men's events at home were not much older than me. These were all muscly, hard, proper *men* with crew cuts, no body hair because they shaved it all off, perfect outsized Greek gods like all those statues in the Stadio dei Marmi next door.

'Well,' I said eventually. I couldn't afford to sit in the sun any longer. 'Once more unto the breech, Mrs C . . .' Mr Jack's carefully typed schedule stipulated a mile and a half today, but I'd be lucky to get in half that. 'Chin up,' she said. I gave her the gold chain with the single pearl I always wore, all I had left of Andy, and slunk down to the concourse in my wrinkly black togs, a pale grey slug, an impostor.

No one was watching; everyone was watching. I found a slim space at the edge of the pool, as far away as I could get from Dawn Fraser. I'd swim in the same event in nine days' time. The nerve! The exhilaration of my first swim had gone. Today I felt heavy and sluggish, a boring little junior strayed into the wrong race. Every length, weaving through the bodies, seemed about a mile long.

I was hanging on the side at the end of my first quarter when someone surged up close by doing breaststroke. Male, tall, panting with hands on hips and looking at me. 'You must be Alex of the Antipodes.'

He was one of those smooth, hard men. From the pale skin,

the accent, and the Union Jack on the bathing cap he was taking off to reveal longish fair hair, an English one.

'Why must I?'

'Because you're wearing the silver fern and the black of your truly marvellous All Blacks . . .'

'I'm wearing the black of the New Zealand Olympic team, if you don't mind.'

'And because you're the only New Zealand swimmer. You have a respectable 63.8 hundred free to your credit, and have therefore been considered a possible finalist. Your rival Maggie Benton was also selected but is alas recuperating from peritonitis. You are, I see, still suffering the effects of your unenviable air journey from New Zealand.'

'Anything else?'

Grandly sweeping back his hair, he bestowed on me a dazzling smile. 'Meet me after training and we'll swop notes. Over a cappuccino and a piece of torte.'

I had thought I was boring, a mere anonymous kid! Yet here was this handsome British hunk with a very posh voice smoothly summing me up. His information was remarkably up to date, God knows where from. He was the same type as Andy. Too smooth, too fast, and too soon.

'Are you chatting me up?'

'Ah, you antipodeans! So amusingly direct. Since you ask, Alex, yes.'

'You don't waste any time. I always thought the English were slow. Gentlemen. Who didn't rush . . .'

'We are, we don't,' he laughed, lying through his handsome teeth. 'I'm Matthew, by the way. Twice British breaststroke champion, current record-holder. I'm reading History at London. I play squash for my college, chess, and know good wines from bad. I've just taken up gliding.'

'You mean those planes with long wings and no engines?'

'Exactly.'

A paragon, but mad, in other words. 'I've someone, at home. Doing engineering, not a swimmer . . .'

'We're in Rome, aren't we?' They talk about women giving seductive smiles! But why had I said that much, why had I off the top of my head, conveniently described Keith as my 'someone'? He'd be pleased, no doubt, very!

'For the Olympics,' I said priggishly, with finality. I climbed out and paused only momentarily on the starting block, aware of scrutiny from below as I called to Bulldog to time me. 'Quarter, 90 percent effort.'

From all the Esther Williams types in the pool, it was *me* he'd chatted up. Nothing like a handsome guy making a pass to make you feel somewhat less like a slug, even if you've decided you can do without boyfriends. Later he swam alongside for several lengths, fast bobbing breaststroke, but he wasn't there when I finished. I didn't see him again, and (mostly) didn't want to. What was torte, anyway? And how the heck did he know about Maggie and her peritonitis?

I managed to get in my mile and a half, change without speaking to anyone other than a hi! to a couple of Australians. Under her umbrella, Bulldog was chatting with the Aussie chaperone like long-lost pals. The Aussies were pretty worried, it seemed, by some of the reports coming from the American camp. Dawn Fraser knew she was going to have to tramp to beat Chris Von Saltza in the hundred free, and John Devitt likewise to beat Lance Larson in the men's event.

'Who was that young man, Alex?' said Bulldog.

'A Brit, no one,' I said sharply. She surely wasn't going to vet every single person I spoke to?

'Sorry to hear about your mate Maggie,' said the Aussie to me, in a voice like an Australian version of Donald Duck. 'I saw her up in Townsville. Promising lass. I hope she goes on next summer after this knock. You any good?'

I was trying to think of a suitably jocular reply when I saw Dawn Fraser get out of the pool and look as though she might be heading our way. 'Sorry, um, just remembered, lunchtime, got to meet someone, Mr Upjohn, some reporter, gotta go, come on Mrs C.' I headed off across the terracotta paving. Bulldog caught me up by the main gate, grumbling in her beard that she didn't know what I was talking about, she wished Mr Upjohn would keep her better informed and she'd love to have met Dawn Fraser. Well, I wouldn't. I had to meet Dawn Fraser sometime, but not today, not yet. I'd had enough excitement for one day.

It was only when I was sitting in the bus going back to the village that the full impact of the three words hit me. 'A respectable 63.8 to your credit. You've been described as a possible finalist.' That was what he said, my pommie history-reading friend. By who? Where? When? A possible *finalist*? Really? You're *nuts*, whoever said that. Go on, pull the other one.

Alex Archer, Olympic Finalist. Well, why not?

If I thought the new Olympic stadium was grand and vast and overwhelming, I ain't seen nuffink yet. We'd driven past the Colosseum on Saturday when we arrived, but no amount of Latin books or guidebooks or postcards could have warned me just what it would be like when you walk towards it as the Romans would have done.

'You should be resting, Alex,' Bulldog grizzled from under her baby-blue umbrella. 'We both should be resting, in this heat. You should have put something with sleeves on. You'll be getting sunburnt. You're already peeling, look, your shoulders. You're a naughty girl, you should have brought a hat. Alex, please slow *down.*'

We were halfway up the Via dei Fori Imperiali, dancing round slow, dawdling tourists who were getting in our way. The Colosseum sat planted at the end of the road, getting bigger with each step. Bulldog moaned on.

'We shouldn't have got off the bus so soon. A free bus too.' We'd waved our identity cards happily at the driver, and got off at the Piazza Venezia, by that ugly great white thing called the Victor Emmanuel II monument. 'Can't you walk a little slower, Alex?'

'Mrs C, don't you realize where we *are?*'

'Of course, but . . .'

'The Via dei Fori Imperiale, down there, look, the Forum, Julius Caesar walked up that street, the Via Sacra, Mark Antony stood on those steps, just *think.*' I knew she was regretting that she'd allowed herself to be hauled out of her siesta to go sightseeing, when only tourists were silly enough to be walking around. I thought teachers would be interested in history.

'You'll be the death of me, Alex,' she grumbled. 'It's not right. You'll never catch up on your sleep at this rate, never mind me, and I don't have to swim.'

'You can sleep when you get home, Mrs C. Now is now.'

We had one more wide crescent of road to negotiate, which nearly saw the end of the Bulldog. While I was gazing dumbstruck at the sheer size of the Colosseum, she forgot yet again that the traffic comes from the other side. She looked the wrong way and very nearly stepped under a bus. The driver threw on the brakes and all his passengers got jolted forward out of their seats. Bulldog scuttled back to the kerb. A Kiwi bus driver would have muttered a bit about bloody tourists, but this one put his head out the window and really yelled at us and waved his arms around. Bulldog was now rattled as well as grumpy, and the driver overacting so much that I yelled back 'You'd probably do the same if you came to our country and people wouldn't scream and shout and rave on at you.' Before he had time to sit down and put his bus into gear I grabbed her elbow and marched her firmly across the road, looking the bus driver in the eyes, daring him to move, just remembering halfway that traffic came from the right, not the left. Even so, my head swivelled to the left out of sheer habit.

Rome was a hot and dangerous place. We'd arrived at the Colosseum.

Later, I remembered noticing Tom outside the crowded entrance, among all the tourist buses, the tourists, horses, horse-dung, souvenir and gelato stalls, balloons, flags, and traffic flying past. It might have been the hat. Just another young Roman, black sunglasses, not quite tall enough to be really elegant. A white linen jacket was slung casually over his shoulders in a way that would be considered highly dubious at home; black linen shirt, sharp white trousers; but the wide straw boater banded in shocking pink was definitely flashy, even by Italian standards.

He was standing by the stalls that sold postcards and slides and cheap-'n-nasty miniatures of the Discus Thrower and Michelangelo's David. As Bulldog stopped to have a look,

43

something about the angle of the hat told me that he was listening, and had read on my shoulder bag that I was in some way connected with the New Zealand team for the Olympic Games, Rome 1960. He didn't look up, as most Romans did (I knew already) to leer at my tallness; yet I do remember that uncomfortable, vague feeling you're being watched, until . . .

I was standing there, just inside the entrance, sheltering from the blinding sun, from the busloads of yabbering pushing tourists, feeling very queasy. We'd walked slowly around the great oval. The jagged remains of the basement area where they kept the animals gaped at me like a mouthful of rotten teeth. The Colosseum could seat fifty thousand people, Bulldog read out. For the opening festivities in AD 80, nine thousand wild beasts and two thousand gladiators were killed. Sometimes they filled the arena with water and had naval battles. They let loose tigers, elephants, crocodiles, lions, hippos, gladiators, and Christians. Teased them and killed them all for pure pleasure. Our guidebook showed a model reconstruction with the tiers of empty seats and the oval sandy arena bare and waiting for blood. I could hear the crowd roaring, hungry.

Bulldog was sitting in a shaded alcove, fanning herself, complaining about sore feet and badly needing a drink. I wanted to go too; but something about the place was holding me; I was hating it, but fascinated too. She was weary enough to give me grudging permission to walk around once by myself. I had ten minutes.

Alone, it got worse. I weaved in and out of these great archways, noticing more than a few scraggly half-dead cats lying round, and found myself going up a steep flight of uneven steps. A surly ticket seller wanted me to buy a ticket. The view from the higher tier was even more eerie. I noticed a large but pathetic white cross below me. Bizarre. Terrified gladiators and animals had waited in those gaping tunnels. The crowd noises in my head got louder and the weight of this whole magnificent horrible place became heavier and I knew I had to get out.

People got in the way. I nearly tripped over two cats and down the steep flight of steps, and completely lost my sense of direction. I walked fast round some groups of people and rudely in front of others taking photographs. I passed a Roman

44

crackpot giving a speech across the arena, to no one. The entrance must be where all the people were. 'Alex, *wait*,' I heard behind me.

Crowds blocked the entrance, slowed my escape. I didn't mean to react at all; well, no more than deliver a fierce glare. I knew about bottom-pinching. It was supposed to be a sign of Roman approval, accepted in good humour. But this wasn't a genial squeeze in the fleshy bit. This was a good, hard nip near my hip bone. I turned furiously, stumbled on the uneven stones, overbalanced, my arms flew out — so it appeared that I'd hit one of a group of obviously Italian youths, right where it hurt.

It's just not the sort of thing which ever happens in New Zealand. Here I was, two days in Rome, and starting a riot. The boys, greasy Elvis carbon copies, were coming at me, three of them, angry — the one I'd hit the angriest. I heard Italian, molto forte and obviously not polite, and saw their hands holding cigarettes making threatening gestures towards my face. I saw puzzled tourists staring blankly at me, wondering what on earth I could have done.

A fourth young man appeared on the scene, as well dressed as the others were sleazy. The black shirt and sunglasses, white linen jacket, the boater with the bright pink ribbon hanging off it. He must have asked what's the problem, because instantly he became the focus of their abuse. The only word I recognized was inglese. 'I'm not inglese and it was an accident,' I shouted back, because now I was getting a bit mad myself. I hadn't started it. The man in the boater put a soothing hand on my arm. 'Un momento! Da dove vieni?' 'What?' 'La Svezia? La Germania? L'Olanda? Australia?' 'Oh-strarr-lia!' I choked. 'Okay, la Nuova Zelanda,' he said, in a voice like chocolate sauce. Then, to the curious crowd, he proceeded to give what I can only describe as an aria. It was like a crowd scene in a musical where the hero comes on and sings and the chorus has to look interested, as though they haven't heard it fifty thousand times before. I stood and gaped, and watched the anger seep out of the faces of the three Italians. From the suave torrent of Italian I picked up only La Grande Olimpiade, Nuova Zelanda, la signorina, giornalista.

It was all over in a minute or two. The youths began to bow

and scrape, offer handshakes which a stern nod from my protector told me I'd be wise to accept. Bulldog found her voice and suggested shakily that we leave. My protector, close enough for a whiff of Old Spice or something similar, took my hand, no kidding, and kissed it, looking up at me with such a wicked gleam in the large brown eyes above the sunglasses I knew immediately we'd be wise to leave, now. I might have jumped out of the frying pan . . . I waited till he'd let go and said, haughtily, without smiling, 'Molte grazie, signor.' 'Prego,' he said, obviously amused at my attempt to freeze him off. We got outside the main entrance and I led Bulldog a merry dance around the gelato stalls, the horses and the Discus Throwers, but we were still followed. I turned around, wondering if my phrase book told me how to tell an Italian to get lost. But he beat me to it. In the split second I took to find any words at all, he took off his sunglasses and grinned.

'Gidday, Kiwi,' he said.

The greater disguise

It has been an eventful day. Historical, even.

I began this morning greatly regretting my decision to come to Rome this week. I've grown used to the leisurely walking pace of Italians around their cities, but here one can walk only at the uncertain dawdle of tourists consulting maps, taking pictures and generally constituting a continual obstacle race to ordinary pedestrians. I caught a bus to the Piazza del Campidoglio, which seemed as good a place as any to begin my explorations, had not all the world's tourists also had the same idea.

Well, I suppose this was always part of it, the Ancient Olympics where people travelled over barren hills for months to get to the Vale of Olympia; once there, they lived cheek by jowl, bought their food from an army of camp followers, stood all day around the stadium in the burning sun to watch the events and lined the rocky pathways to watch the processions. Here, one can at least escape into a bar at regular intervals. As I walked up the Via dei Fori Imperiali, I pondered the idea of looking up one of my Milanese contacts, to pursue the offer of a battered Vespa, which raises the question of whether sun-stroked tourists or Roman traffic is the greater challenge.

There was no mistaking the tall girl, standing with her dumpy chaperone on the kerb, about to cross over to the Colosseum, shouting angrily at a bus driver. I'd heard a screech of brakes. I looked across to see a nearby bus bounce back on its springs and the driver leaning out the window being remarkably abusive, as only Italians can. I remember my own confusion when I first walked around Milan, the constant danger of traffic hurtling at you from the left. Few people would take on Roman

47

bus drivers or Roman traffic other than foolhardy locals, but this girl did. Having momentarily quelled the bus driver, she marched across the road, holding up the flow of traffic by sheer will-power, dragging her companion by the hand.

Presumably, Alexandra Archer and chaperone, going to visit the Colosseum.

The coincidence I do not find, in retrospect, so very strange. We both arrived on Saturday. A day of rest — she may be a churchgoer, a Roman Catholic? — then one of the first choices for sightseeing would naturally be the Colosseum. She would probably have spent the morning training, as I spent some time practising, learning some more of my *Figaro* score.

The greater disguise today was the linen jacket slung as Italians do, over the shoulders. (It appears my absent landlady has a peripatetic son who uses the apartment as his Roman base; handily, he is about the same build as me, with a flamboyant and expensive taste in clothes; I shall have anything I borrow dry-cleaned.) I digress — back to the Colosseum — supposedly examining the Italian guidebooks, I caught a glimpse of her airline bag inscribed with New Zealand Olympic Games Rome 1960. She took charge of buying an English guidebook, clearly several steps ahead of her shaken companion in dealing with lire and stall-keepers. She was not wearing uniform, but an unremarkable cotton skirt, striped in beige and turquoise, white blouse, probably home-made specially for the trip, sandals, not a trace of cosmetics. I saw the pink of new sunburn on her winter-pale shoulders and arms; she caught me looking and glared. Before I moved away, I heard an unusually low-pitched voice, telling her chaperone to stop looking at postcards and come and look at the real thing. I heard, Alex.

I followed them discreetly, giving thanks for the long sight which runs in the family. My own reaction to the Colosseum was coloured by watching her, even from twenty yards, register first disbelief at its size, and then a growing repugnance. I saw her wrap her arms around herself as though cold, even though the temperature must have been approaching a hundred in the shade. She stood for a long time in one shaded alcove, as though listening, and later I saw her looking down at the white cross, as though marvelling at its incongruity in that barbaric place; discordant it certainly is. Then she began walking, quite fast for the heat, around the upper circle. I lost her, so made for the main entrance only to hear some raised voices: a disturbance, and an angry young New Zealander at the centre of it, standing her ground against a group of three or four hostile Italian youths.

I could either be an uncomprehending Italian bystander and let her sort it out for herself, or reveal myself as an interpreter, or a fellow Kiwi gone italiano, or . . .

Rome was not built in a day, Tom.

Tommaso

'Just how long can you keep this up?' I asked, exasperated to the point of wanting to scream. 'What about me? And the Bulldog, who's about as green as they come, so square she's cubic. You can't for much longer.'

'I can, for as long as I choose,' said Tom. 'And you can. Mrs Churchill will keep it up because she thinks I'm rather a lad. She's a good sort who likes a bit of fun.'

'It's going on too long. I think you're a poser and a fake.' That amused Tom greatly. 'I don't like covering up for fakes, having to keep acting a part, a lie, really.'

'Don't you, Alex?,' he said, feigning surprise. 'I thought you were doing it rather well.'

Four days after the Colosseum, five days before the opening ceremony, several things were driving me mad.

One, the heat had got beyond a joke. It was now officially a heat-wave, the worst for decades. At least the swimmers were the best off, by far, for training. Two, being in Rome and barred from sightseeing was torture. And three, Tomas Alexander was driving me absolutely bananas and he'd got beyond a joke too.

He was now established as Tommaso, the unofficial honorary self-appointed interpreter to the New Zealand team, on hand daily to sort out any little administrative problems we might have, available for advice on bus timetables, menus, brochures, training times. How he got hold of a press pass to get into village remained a mystery. The trouble was, all our team thought he was an Italian who'd spent some time in Australia and once toured New Zealand, loved 'your *beau*-tiful country' so very much. His papa, he told us all with deep sincerity, his dead papa had been captured by New Zealand soldiers in the

51

war. Had been treated like a gentleman, and got Christmas cards from two of them in Tau*ran*-ga and 'ow you say, Titi*ran*-gi? He pronounced both names with a hard G sound and the accents all wrong, relishing it. Had at his own expense come down to Rome from Milan, where he worked in a travel bureau, to see if he could be of help. Our team men goggled at his hats and sharp clothes, which every day were different, and grinned tolerantly when he arrived during breakfast and went round *Buon giorno, signorina, signora!,* kissing the hands of all the women in the team — mine in an offhanded way, and the Bulldog's warmly. His English was 'ow you say? stilted, with bad grammar and a sing-song accent, frequently breaking in frustration into Italian. They all thought he was Italian bloody marvellous.

Whereas — Bulldog and I knew otherwise. What do you do when a dashing Italian with gorgeous brown eyes, who apparently can't speak a word of English, rescues you from hostile locals about to punch you in the face, then comes out with 'Gidday, Kiwi'? You assume he's an I-tie trying to be smart?

You'd be wrong. Under the linen jacket and pink ribbon he was all solid Kiwi, originally from a farm near Taihape, more recently from four years at Auckland University would you believe? Walking back along the Via dei Fori Imperiali, and over my first experience of gelato and a very small aperitivo in a bar near the Piazza Venezia, we learnt that he was living in Milano. He'd been there for eighteen months, studying Italian. He'd come to Rome for the Games. He seemed more interested in asking about us, the team, what was I competing in. Who was going to win the New Zealand elections in November and whether the Twist had reached there yet! How would I know, when I hadn't been to a single dance all year, not since Andy died.

Why, I asked, had he passed himself off as Italian? 'Because I've been speaking nothing but Italian for eighteen months. I've worked hard at it. I wanted to see if the locals could pick an accent. They didn't, at least not a foreign one. It was necessary to dress like an Italian too, down to the sideburns, the eau-de-cologne. 'The rest,' he said, with a chilling smile, 'is pure wickedness, with a touch of revenge thrown in. Kiwi blokes are generally rather humourless. It amuses me that they'll accept flamboyance from an Italian, but not, I don't doubt, from a Kiwi.'

I asked him what he'd said to the youths at the Colosseum.

'That you were an athlete from New Zealand . . .'

'How did you know?'

'I read it on your shoulder bag, earlier. You were here in Rome for the Games. They should be understanding of people who spoke no Italian. You came from a country where harrassing and touching a young woman was considered most anti-social and unacceptable behaviour. That I was a journalist from Milan working for the international press. I would hate to report that young Romans were making life unpleasant for their Olympic visitors. Have another aperitivo, Mrs Churchill. Alessandra, try some cassata!'

Honestly!

Four days later I thought the joke was wearing a bit thin and told him so. He joined the team for most meals, and often came with me to afternoon training where he flashed the press card about. He had stamina and he didn't overact. My team-mates were totally hoodwinked. He was discreet Italian charm itself, not a false Kiwi note anywhere; except once, when he slipped and fell heavily on wet tiles as we were leaving the pool and swore, though softly, in very full-blooded Kiwi. We never saw him without a hat.

I found myself at breakfast each morning watching the dining hall doorway for his arrival. I felt resentful when he was collared by one of the managers and spirited off to do something useful. He never once looked at me as he left, indeed he rather ignored me, but I somehow knew that he was saying 'back soon' to me. By the weekend, with the Games opening next Thursday, I was becoming highly frustrated that it was Tommaso the fake Italian I was seeing most of the time, the genuine Kiwi article only coming and going to the pool with me and Mrs Churchill.

He said he was living near the Terme di Caracalla, in an apartment belonging to the aunt of a Milanese friend who'd fled to Scotland at the doubly appalling prospect of an August heat wave *and* the Olympic Games. I couldn't imagine any circumstances in which I'd be allowed to see him alone.

53

Bulldog was like a leech. Perhaps he didn't want to see me specially.

Sightseeing in that heat was out. Bulldog and I had come back so exhausted from our Monday afternoon trip to the Colosseum, full of cassata and aperativos, that Mr Upjohn had issued an Edict: there'd be no more sightseeing for me until after my events were over.

Though it was terrible to be in Rome and seeing nothing, I knew he was right. By the time I did my early training and had breakfast, it was half past ten and already too hot and too late to go catching buses into the city. Everything took longer in the heat. You tried not to, but you just got slower. I spent the mornings writing letters home, wandering round the village shops, trying not to think of my race in a few days, trying not to hope that Tom Alexander would come round the next corner. His services were in demand elsewhere.

Lunch late as possible, at 1.30 or even 2.00, long siesta tossing on hot sheets, in the bus to go training again at 4.30. Wander back over the bridge in the yellow light, leisurely dinner, early bed. The swimming events were all in the first week; I had a week afterwards to see Rome. Sunday would be the exception, when the Pope was to give a special audience for the Olympic athletes in St Peter's square. We'd all be going, in full uniform of course.

The only good thing about training was Tom sometimes sitting up in the stands, under his own large golfer's umbrella. Most of the time I felt heavy and tired. It was taking me longer to get over the trip than I thought. Some ning-nong might have said 'a possible finalist', but I still felt like a silly junior amongst all those strong, gorgeous bodies. I identified some of the other freestylers I'd be swimming against. They all looked so effortless, fast. English Matthew made a couple more passes, then gave me up as a bad job and turned his attentions to one of the Aussies. Apparently he'd read about me in an English swimming magazine, previewing prospects for the Games. A possible finalist, an outside chance. Not bloody likely; my times, when I could get in a complete time trial without having to swerve around someone, were *awful*. Mr Jack's notes, which I opened day by day, told me to expect this, not to worry. By then, he had written, 'Day 4, 3, 2, you must concentrate on speedwork, starts, turns, rest. Day 1 will be the opening ceremony. Relax and enjoy it, conserve your energy. D-day, think only of your race plan.'

I was thinking more and more of Tom. None of the others, preoccupied with their own training, knew he was coming to the pool to watch my sessions, even Zoe who told me daily what a *dish* he was, 'that Italian guy with his hats. I think he quite fancies me,' she said. 'Lucky you,' I said.

Oh for a simple life! Instead, count-down training, an attack of diarrhoea, restless and sweating at night, again dreaming of crowds, animals, blood, races where I ran and ran and ran and moved not an inch, while something nameless and dreadful got closer.

On Saturday afternoon (four days to the opening ceremony) a familiar face turned up at the pool. My friend Norm Thompson from the *Herald*, just arrived from New Zealand, looking very old and very tired. He'd not told me he was coming to Rome; he said he didn't know himself until ten days ago. He brought letters and news from Mum and Dad, letters with pictures from Debbie and Robbie and even Jamie, from Gran with a pressed flower inside, from Mr Jack. Everyone was fine. It'd done nothing but rain since I left.

Last week, he heard that Maggie was going to live in Australia as soon as she was completely better, ending our rivalry of many years. She was finished with swimming, said Norm. I looked at all the bodies churning up and down the pool and wondered, for each one of those, how many hundreds were there like Maggie? Those who cocked up the one crucial race that mattered, or got peritonitis five days before leaving. Who missed the bus for a big Games and wouldn't go on asking for punishment. Oh Maggie my friend, you should have been here. You deserved it. It's not fair.

And how did I find the pool, asked Norm, getting out his notebook wearily. A fast pool? Turning ends good? Those yellow lane markers looked pretty substantial — could I see over them? How was my training going? Time trials? How was I coping with the heat? The rich food? Sleeping okay? And first international competition, how was I feeling about that? Missing my coach? Did I feel prepared? Any injuries, pulled muscles, ligaments, eye troubles? My chances? Would sub-64 win me a place in the semi-final? Apart from Fraser and Von Saltza, who were the threats? Did I feel intimidated by these vast stands? How did I think I'd feel, when it came to standing on those starting blocks?

Well, I'm used to being interviewed, and Norm had always been on my side. Mean or not, I didn't tell him about 'a possible finalist', though. I knew enough about the sort of thing reporters wrote, even (or especially) Norm. I could just see it. U.K. EXPERTS PICK ALEX ARCHER FOR ROME FINAL. Anyway, it was codswallop.

I got the impression that Tom, though he'd been only casually introduced to Norm as our honorary interpreter, was all ears as he gazed across the pool. 'I'm filing my first piece tonight, if I can stay awake that long,' said Norm. 'Update on you and the runners, Halberg and co. They need something at home to balance the hysteria coming out of South Africa.' The country, he said, was in a ferment over the fourth and deciding test being played against the Springboks next Saturday. Well, a virtual world title was at stake.

'How incredibly dreary,' muttered Tom, then remembering, 'Rug-bee, not — 'ow you say? — a patch on zee football.' Was that Tom or Tommaso speaking? Norm, it appeared, had turned down an offer to cover the South African tour. Unlike all his colleagues, he said, he believed the protesters — 'people like you, Alex' — would turn out to be right. 'I couldn't go, could I, thinking that?' I saw Tom's eyes flicker. 'You are protester, Alex?' he said. 'Si,' I said. 'Congratulazioni!' He turned to Bulldog who was sitting fanning herself drowsily, smiling at Tommaso.

'Domani, Signora, posso — can I?' He looked up at the hazy white-blue sky. 'No, there really comes a point.'

He'd cracked. I loved it. Norm Thompson's eyes popped out of his head as Tom went on, 'All that talk of home, and the bloody All Blacks. It's nostalgia in reverse.'

'Home?' said Norm. 'I thought you were a dinkum I-tie.' Bulldog was now awake, chuckling away heartily.

'You're a journalist. You don't reveal your sources,' said Tom bluntly. 'At the Olympic village, I'm from Milan, the team's honorary interpreter and general factotum. I work in a travel bureau. My father was taken prisoner-of-war by New Zealanders in Libya. I learned my English in Australia. I once went to New Zealand, your beautiful country,' this in stage Italian English, the vowels stretched out like chewing-gum. 'I bumped into these good ladies at the Colosseum. Alex was in trouble, being threatened by hostile elements.'

'What's new?' asked Norm, drily. 'Packet of trouble, always was. What had she done?'

'Been pinched by a randy Roman and retaliated,' said Tom.

'Oh dear, yes, she would,' laughed Norm.

'This man's a fake,' I said. 'He comes from Taihape. He likes charades.'

'I intend to keep up this charade, to the end of your stay,' said Tom with a warning edge to his voice. 'If they find out, the men especially, they'll go for me. Good Kiwi jokers don't go in for fancy dress, charades, tricks on their mates. Not one that goes on for three weeks. I'd be labelled a cheat, impostor, all the way through to camp as a row of tents, which I'm not. Especially if they knew what I was really doing here.'

'What are you doing here?' I asked curiously.

'Learning Italian. And singing.' He turned to Bulldog. 'Can I take Alessandra for lunch tomorrow, after the Pope's junket? It will be very leisurely. I know an excellent restaurant, clean and quiet. I promise to have her back by four, in a taxi, in good time for training. I'll see that she eats the right things and not too much. You'll say yes?'

Clever Tom, he'd anticipated all her conditions. How could she say anything else? The child could go.

The trattoria was in a small piazza not far from St Peter's, with tables set up on the pavement outside. He'd obviously booked, because we were shown to the only remaining table, and the best one, in a corner shaded by trees and a dazzling bougainvillaea, exactly the same pinky-red as the one climbing over our verandah at home. I was surrounded by greenery and things pink: the waiters' pink aprons matched the tablecloths. There were pink roses on the tables and fuchsias hanging above us, and there sat Tom in a pink shirt (cyclamen, as in Gran's favourite pot plant) and his Colosseum boater with the pink band, almost as if he'd planned to match up with it all.

'I thought *Karachi* was hot,' I said as we collapsed onto our pink wooden chairs. A polite old waiter came and took my hat and blazer away. They don't do that at home. I was feeling very dowdy and gawky in my grey uniform skirt and white shirt which was sticking to my back. My nose was peeling horribly. The pool was my territory. This was his. He'd said very little since we left the team behind in St Peter's square and slowly walked about a quarter of a mile down empty streets with everything closed up, marvellous heavy doors, shutters, shop windows. It was a nice silence, though, just the sound of our feet on the cobblestones and occasional music or voices from an apartment five stories above. At this time of the day people were either eating lunch or already sleeping.

He had a brisk exchange with the waiter, while I drank all the water on the table. Bottles of beer and orange juice and a basket of thick holey bread arrived almost immediately. It was the first time we'd been alone and face to face. He carefully poured the beer, but he'd taken off his sunglasses and was looking at me. I took refuge in looking round at the families behind me, eight or ten at a table, with toddlers whose chins poked just over the table, eating and talking with gusto. My family had never ever been out to a restaurant together, Gran, Debbie, everyone . . .

'Your orange juice, signorina.' When I looked back at Tom, the boater had gone. For the first time in a week he was hatless, studying the menu but clearly waiting for the inevitable reaction. With the cyclamen shirt, the bougainvillaea behind, the effect was spectacular.

'Why do you cover it up?' I said finally.

'People can't take their eyes off it. Even now.' A quick glance behind me confirmed what he meant. 'People don't believe it's natural. As a child it was corn blond. Most people's hair goes darker and duller. My late grandmother was Irish, curse her Belfast bones. They still talk about her hair, in Taihape.'

'I'm not surprised. Is that what you call Titian?'

'Among other things. I've worn hats since I was in prep school. My trademark. Like Edith Sitwell.' He parodied the supercilious pose I remembered from a book about English poetry, making me laugh. 'Hats save me from the knobbly fingers of old crones accosting me in shops. And they do, believe me.'

It wasn't only the incredible colour, which the patchy sunlight through the trees was setting alight with streaks of copper and gold. It was wavy and very thick, and longer than any Kiwi short back 'n sides. It explained the bronzy eyebrows, the coppery freckles which had made me wonder earlier whether his hair might be reddish, and all the hats. Used to being stared at myself, I could understand the hats. His level gaze was very disconcerting. I took a long swig of orange juice.

'What was the Pope talking about?' I asked.

'The usual platitudes — brotherhood of nations in friendly rivalry and so forth. But that was quite a special occasion, make no mistake. Usually he appears at an upstairs balcony.'

The Pope and his party in gorgeous reds and magentas and purples on a bright blue stage in front of St Peter's, the dome and columns and statues above us, the square packed with all the Games athletes in their uniforms, and tourists and pigeons, the morning heat, the amplified single old voice, the bells at the end — I had stood feeling totally dwarfed. 'It was amazing,' I said lamely. 'Makes New Zealand look . . .'

'Don't compare this with home, Alex,' he said sharply. 'This place has two thousand years of history. Ours is only just beginning. Though God knows I couldn't get out fast enough.'

'Why?'

'Alex, Alessandra, let's get this bit over,' he said, dodging the question and picking up the menu. 'Then we can relax and enjoy our lunch.'

With the waiter hovering, I thought he meant helping me choose from the long and rather dog-eared menu. I recognized a few words — spaghetti, scaloppine, gelato — but what on earth were calamari, verdure di stagione, fritto misto? 'I think I'll need some help.'

'I don't mean this.' He said a few words in Italian which sent the waiter sidling away. 'I've decided to go away for a few days. It'll be a week.'

I again took refuge in the menu, knowing I was being

watched. 'Oh?' I said casually. 'I thought you'd come to see the Games.'

'And Rome. That was the original intention, yes.'

'You've been very . . . translating and stuff.' Why couldn't I talk proper? 'The managers need, well, little things . . .' Even that morning, there'd been a muddle with the bus. It was Tommaso, with much hand-waving and shrugging, who'd calmed down the officials and sorted it out.

'They'll cope,' he said. 'There are interpreters in the village, on tap.'

'Yes, but . . .'

'I am recalled to my ufficio, urgente.'

'Any more of that Italian accent, I'll scream. You don't work in an office.'

'You're sure about that?' he said slyly. No, damn it, I wasn't sure of anything about him, nor why I should be feeling so let down. Six days, then he just ups and leaves.

'After my . . .'

'For a performer there's only the here and now,' he said gently. 'Tonight's performance, or in your case Thursday's first and most important race. You can't afford to think of after. It seems to me that as an Olympic athlete you're required to be a performer, a professional.'

'I am not,' I said indignantly, recalling past slurs on my reputation, evil attempts to have me declared not an amateur.

'You are in the classical Greek sense.'

'I'm at — I'm a student more hours than I train.'

'You're being supported to pursue your sport, just as Greek athletes were by their city-states.'

'Only temporarily. It's cost my parents a bomb.'

'You may not get actual money, but if you succeed . . .'

'Let's see. A Hollywood film contract, the second Esther Williams. Offer of a scholarship to an American university. Three cheers in assembly at . . .' Again I stopped short of saying school. I didn't want him to know I was still at school. 'Where's all this leading?'

'How old are you?'

I wondered how much Bulldog had told him.

'Eighteen, nearly nineteen. And you?'

'Twenty-three. Could you still be around at the next Olympics?'

'Possibly,' I said playing for time. 'You've been sitting with Bulldog at training, what did she say?'

His slow smile acknowledged the loaded question and the possible advantage of knowing a good deal more about me than I about him. My age, for starters. 'Not much,' he said, too lightly to be the truth. 'But I've listened to you, and that reporter, and watched you training. I had no idea what was involved. That's what I mean, you have a professional's attitude. That's why I'm leaving you to it.'

I must still have looked puzzled and unconvinced.

'If *I* was preparing for my international début . . . well, you just don't need any distractions.'

'Distractions.' I played with my knife on the pink tablecloth, feeling very much on the back foot. 'Presuming?'

'Rather a lot, I know. That we might have enjoyed exploring Rome together.' Ah, he was backing off until my events were over. I was on my own. Again. Our eyes met briefly. 'Most of my time has been spent in Milan.'

'Where you're studying singing?'

He nodded, but didn't seem inclined to enlighten me further. He signalled the waiter over. We went through the elaborate business of translating, explaining, deciding on antipasto for both, followed by fish grilled in a special Roman style, peperoni, and verdura mista. A white chianti — I thought chianti was always red. I had the feeling that the previous five minutes had been vaguely unsatisfactory. What did he expect me to say: see ya later, alligator? or, please stay, I need your dry humour to get me through this week, someone under sixty and sane outside the team? Someone to raise a little cheer for the New Zealand team of one when she stands up in front of that monstrous crowd next Friday afternoon.

'Nevertheless,' he said, when we returned to the table with our platefuls of antipasto, 'I shall be sad not to see you swim.'

'And the opening ceremony. Pity. You're going back to Milan?'

He seized, I thought with some relief, on the subject of Milan. Through the antipasto, the mussels and peppers and pesce, the whole slow fantastic lunch, he treated me to the glories of

Milan, the Gothic cathedral, the arcades, fashions, cake shops, the Lombardy plains and the lakes not far away. Most of all the opera house, La Scala, where he watched performances with other students from high up in the sixth tier. He was boarding with a large family: Papa was a teacher, and three women — Mama, Nonna, and Nonna's younger sister Carla — together ruled the family of five sons and two daughters with a great deal of noise. It was very cheap because Nonna had a soft spot for aspiring singers, but difficult to get peace or privacy. From various teachers he was learning singing, musicology, theory, opera history, Greek and Roman history, stagecraft, movement, fencing. His main singing teacher was a noted baritone, his fencing master a former European champion, now a nimble fifteen stone, cunning as a fox and still unbeatable. Then he got onto Florence, the only other city he'd spent any time in. I listened, and sipped my white chianti, and tried to eat as slowly as he was (since he was doing all the talking), and basked in the pink warmth of it all.

'And now Roma, La Città Eterna,' he said as the waiter put minute cups of black coffee in front of us. 'Don't be deceived by the tiny cups. It's thick and powerful and all you need. I've got two weeks here.'

'But you're leaving.'

'Where I go is beside the point.' His eyes were on his coffee as he said, 'Alessandra, you're within three days of your life's ambition. I'll not ever have it said that some expatriate Kiwi arrived in Rome and . . .' A long silence hung between us.

'You've got a press pass, haven't you?' I asked softly.

'So I have.' He smiled and somehow, putting on his hat adjusting the angle of his pink collar, he turned into an Italian before my very eyes. In a hilarious mixture of Italian and terrible pidgin English he informed me that his name was Marcello Mastroianni from Milano, lika zee filma starra, lo stesso, ma no lo stesso, capisci? He was a giornalista 'ere in Roma per La Grande Olimpiade, ma specialmente per osservare la Regina della piscina, la bellissima nuotatrice Dawn Fraser dell' Austraaa-lia when she swim i cento metri, 'ow you say, freestyle? also i quattrocento metri freestyle. This was not the discreet Tommaso but the journalist at the Colosseum again. But he was molto arrabbiato ''ow you say, angree — my Eenglish is verra verra bad' because he could not 'geta zee pressa passa per il villaggio Olimpico'.

He was telling me that he would watch me swim from the press box, but would not come near the village for a week, until it was all over.

'Ho-kay, Signorina Archer? he said, taking off his boater and putting it to his chest like a minstrel tap-dancer taking a bow. 'Ho-kay?'

'Ho-kay,' I said.

The cry went up the next morning. 'Where's Tommaso?' Faces around the breakfast table looked blank. 'Anyone seen Tommaso? Someone must've seen our dago ponce.' It was one of the managers, cycling or something, a fat little fellow dashing in, puce in the face, about to have a heart attack.

I held my tongue, metaphorically speaking, and then found I'd done it for real. 'Ouch!' Dago *ponce*! How dare he, going on to all and sundry that one of his boys needed a physio quick-quick and there wasn't a village physio to be found for love nor money, and where had that I-tie gone. 'Yeow.' Heads turned. 'How should I know?' I said savagely. 'I bit my tongue.' There was blood on my bread roll.

I was already in a bad *bad* mood. I'd had to go to early and very crowded training because today at eleven hundred hours there was a compulsory rehearsal for the opening ceremony, where we'd be put in our lines and practise marching, and I'd wanted to see the Olympic Stadium when it was the real cheering thing, not empty.

Zoe, who was nagging me nightly to put my bed light off because *she* wanted to sleep, had been woken at six this morning by Bulldog coming in to wake me and falling over something on the floor, and had gone berserk. English Matthew, out of luck with the Aussie bombshell, so patronizing and clean-cut and confident he made me puke, had made another pass. Someone's fingernail had sliced a 14-inch groove down my thigh. Then the French owner of the red nail came and abused me for getting in her road, and I was too amazed and too slow to point out that I had as much right to pool space as her.

There was no mail from home today. My period was finished, but I was still permanently tired and hot, and my bowel workings permanently odd. My nose and back were peeling badly. I came and went from the changing-room without any one of the females in there saying anything more than 'Hi'. I wasn't so much a small fish in this pond as an invisible one. There'd been no mail for three days.

I had to swim my best race ever on Friday.

After breakfast, with an hour and a half to spare before the marching practice, I propped myself up on my bed and confided in my diary. Written down, it looked like the whingeing of a spoilt brat. Then I wrote up yesterday:

Sunday Went to St Peter's in the morning, saw the Pope, audience for all the Games athletes. Went to a pink restaurant with Tom, tried squid (calamari) and mussels (cozze) and white chianti. Caught a taxi to Borghese Gardens, walked a bit, taxi back to training, felt lousy, tea, bed.

I looked at the bland words. That's what a ten-year-old would write. Come on Alex, you could do better than that. Which Alex? Aye, there's the rub. The one who isn't quite telling the truth most of the time. The one who is feeling totally overwhelmed by everything: the pool, all those fabulous female bodies, officials, the village, Rome, everything? The one who stuttered and stumbled her way through lunch with a young man called Tom yesterday, feeling about thirteen; who accepted his unilateral decision to go away for a few days; too proud and too scared to say please don't, I think I'll swim better with you around.

Why? What did I know about the man, except that he was apparently a Kiwi here learning Italian and singing, with a penchant for playing serious jokes on people, and an amazing head of hair.

He'd given nothing away over lunch, except his present life in Milan. Hints: he came from a farm near Taihape, he'd been to prep school, therefore his parents had money. He'd been to Auckland University and wanted to be an opera singer. He couldn't get out of New Zealand fast enough. Why? He'd not

64

asked me one single question: about my family, what I was doing, school or work, the usual things people want to know about so-called champions. So either he knew it already from Bulldog or some other source, or he wasn't interested in me, just himself and how great and cosmopolitan he was, learning how to be an Italian. I didn't like either thought much.

After the lunch, he'd suggested a short stroll in the Borghese Gardens, as Romans do on a hot Sunday afternoon. We had an hour before I had to be back for training. The taxi took us past the Castel Sant' Angelo, by the river. I recognized it, with the angel on top, from the cover of the long-playing record of *Tosca* we had at home. I didn't tell him I knew the music backwards. I got the full story, how the last act was set on the battlements of the castle, 'up there, look!' How Tosca and her lover both came to a messy end, and the famous story about the soprano who jumped to her death into a mattress sprung like a trampoline and rebounded back into view of the audience. The police chief Scarpia, he said, was one of the best verismo baritone roles written, a scheming sadist with wonderfully oily, melodious music to sing. By Byron's statue at the entrance to the Borghese Gardens, I got a quick run-down on Byron in Italy, and Keats and other Romantic poets who'd also been obsessed with Italy. He read the extracts from *Childe Harold* written in English on the base of the statue, beautifully, like an actor.

> Oh Rome! my country! city of the soul!
> The orphans of the heart must turn to thee,
> Lone mother of dead empires! and control
> In their shut breasts their petty misery.
> What are our woes and sufferance? Come and see
> The cypress, hear the owl, and plod your way
> O'er steps of broken thrones and temples. Ye!
> Whose agonies are evils of a day —
> A world is at our feet as fragile as our clay.

Then followed the Borghese family, the gardens and art collections they'd left to Rome. I don't think he'd swotted all this up or was specially trying to impress me; it welled up from sheer enthusiasm. We walked down dry earthy pathways under the pine trees, past a lake and statues and a small grassy stadium where they were getting ready to have some of the Olympic horse events. There were small groups of boys playing soccer, and young families pushing babies and admiring daughters in gorgeous old-fashioned dresses and black patent-leather shoes. Old men snoozed on the park benches, courting couples walked along with the boy's arm over the girl's shoulder. By a rotunda, children were taking rides in a trap drawn by a Shetland pony. He talked about soccer as Italy's national game, and Italian family life and courting customs, and the Shetland pony he'd once had as a child. The grass was brown and parched and everything a bit overgrown, but it was a park for people. Our parks at home, the Domain or Cornwall Park, seemed too well kept, pretty but empty.

At ten to four, in another taxi outside the village entrance, he thanked me for the day. I thanked him. He wished me luck for Friday. I said thanks. We got out of the taxi and walked to the entrance — now very crowded and busy because, with only three days before the opening ceremony, all the teams had arrived. He said 'Ciao, Alessandra'; I said 'Goodbye, Tom'. He took my hand and kissed it formally, but this time he did not look up. I felt his lips on my hand, just half a second longer than polite. Half a second will be the difference between a gold medal and nothing. Something inside me went 'help'. He walked straight back to the taxi, Tommaso tossing his white jacket over his pink shoulders. At the taxi he turned, and seeing I was still watching, doffed his hat very briefly, so that the last sight I had was a flash of copper.

I wondered if I'd ever see him again.

Present laughter

How my musician friends in Milan would be laughing! I came to Rome primarily to have a break from work and see the city, secondly, to see something of the Games; I have ended up interpreter to the New Zealand team, camp follower at the Olympic village, familiar with the venues for the cycling, the boxing, training venues for the runners, familiar with the Olympic pool and the area around the Piscine Coni, an instant expert on prospects for the women's freestyle events, caught up in the heat and fever of it all.

A giornalista, no less, sporting a smart wardrobe courtesy of my apartment's absent owner and a press pass, gained after some very fast talking to a flustered junior at the New Zealand Embassy and another at the Olympic press office, trading on the respected name of Norman Thompson and his paper.

I cannot believe that Alex is not yet sixteen; a birthday late October, Mrs Churchill said. Her training sessions would cripple an average man, yet she tells me these are light. Tapering off is the expression, I believe. The week has put colour in her face, a light tan on those long legs and across the square shoulders; taken the skin off her longish nose. Among the most wonderful female bodies I have ever seen, she moves — I can think here only in clichés — like a cat, poised, precise, controlled, slightly imperious, distancing herself from the other swimmers, and it has to be said, from me. Some of the other girls appear to flail and fight the water; she goes through it, sleek and rhythmic, beautiful to watch. She swims with the relentless tireless perfection of a Bach fugue. Poetry, no, music in motion. Clichés again.

I think she understands very well the reason why I involved myself with the team. Do I imagine that behind the studied indifference, the unusual and perceptive reaction to my crowning glory revealed . . .? Also, why I have removed myself. Perhaps I should have expected that her response to my announcement of departure would be nonchalance, an air of I can take it or leave it, I have a job to do. Surely I didn't really expect her to collapse in a heap and say, Tom, don't go, I need your support, I'll swim to a gold medal for you! That is the stuff, the corn of light romances. The young woman I saw holding up three lanes of Roman traffic, or bailed up in the Colosseum, needs no one. She would have managed without me, probably shouted some school Shakespeare back at them. I should write here and now: friendship, or romance, will not be won easily.

Contrary to my expectations, I have enjoyed talking with Mrs Churchill and Norm Thompson, watching Alex train. News from home has not been unwelcome, especially as told by Norm, whose job as a sports reporter belies his wide knowledge of what is happening back home. He expects Walter Nash's Labour Government to go out at the end of the year. Television, he says, is coming next year and will transform New Zealand utterly, particularly in view of its isolation. Twenty years hence, elections will be won or lost on television; look at what's happening in the American elections, Kennedy and Nixon's planned TV debates. It's a long way from the rural village meetings I remember as a child, uncle rampant as local chairman.

About Alex, though, both have been curiously reticent; vague references to a rival, one Maggie Benton, to a swimming career not unmarked by injury, problems; not elucidated.

Without my press pass, without our tacit agreement that I'll be watching her swim from the press box, I'm not sure I could have stood it, remaining in Rome knowing that Alessandra was here. I think I should have scuttled back to Milan and buried my head in learning some more Hugo Wolf lieder or 'Das Lied von der Erde' or something equally soulful; saying to hell with her and with the Olympics and let Rome wait for another, less potent, occasion.

Won't it come to this anyway? An airport parting, separation by half a world. Irreconcilable distances, ambitions. Better gently, ruefully, to retire, now?

None shall sleep

Tuesday, Wednesday dragged past. Hiding from the sun, sleeping, writing letters, training only once a day, mostly sprints, dreadful times. Both the main Olympic pool and the nearby indoor pool with the horse murals were crowded now. There was less chat in the changing-room. Bulldog heard rumours there was trouble in the Australian camp, scared to death of the Americans. Their coaches had trouble getting past security guards into the pool. I didn't even *have* a coach. I checked the press box above the starting area for people under forty wearing hats. Niente.

Besides letters from Mum and Gran, a steady trickle of telegrams from all sorts of people started to arrive. Zoe and I didn't have much to say to each other, and the heat had got to Bulldog. About five thousand times a day I thought of standing up on the blocks sometime after three on Friday, and shuddered. I tried not to think of Tom at all. I'd gone into a sort of limbo.

We had a final marching practice, and got issued with bits of paper to tell us the programme for the ceremony. Basically, we marched in behind our flags, stood in the middle of the arena during speeches, anthems, raising the flag, lighting the Olympic flame, then marched out again.

The Olympic flame, our village newsletter told us, had arrived in Rome, carried by 1500 men and boys all the way from the sacred grove at Olympia. Down Greece, across the Adriatic to Sicily on an Italian sailing-ship called the *Amerigo Vespucci*, and up through Italy. Tonight it would be kept alight at the Piazza del Campidoglio designed by Michelangelo. Tomorrow it would be carried at the appointed hour into the stadium by a

71

young athlete, his name kept a secret, Italian and male of course, though I couldn't see whyever not a girl, like Diana or Atalanta in the Greek myths.

Today Mr Upjohn arrived at the pool to give me time trials. Important time trials. Bulldog and I looked at each other and winked. What did he think she and I had been *doing* this past week while he went off to all those managers' meetings or was just generally absent?

After I'd done two lousy 100 metre time trials and some 50 metre sprints down crowded lanes through churned-up water, he put forward the monstrous idea that I should not take part in the opening ceremony tomorrow. It was a long march to the stadium, over two miles; there'd be a lot of standing around. Apparently there were rumours that some people competing on Friday would be resting, not marching.

'You only get the one chance,' he said. 'You think I don't know that?' I said angrily. Below us the American girls had taken over a lane and were lining up for 50 metre sprints, one sleek golden body after another. I just didn't, surely, swim as fast as that. 'If I don't march tomorrow, I don't swim.' He looked startled, opened his mouth to tell me off and decided to grind his teeth instead. Our few exchanges of recent days had been quite friendly.

There was still no significant hat in the press box.

I went into the changing-room after that last session feeling sort of helpless, resigned. It was up to the fates now. I'd done hundreds of miles, twice a day for a year, just about non-stop since my broken leg. If I ever needed a friendly face in the changing-room, it was then.

The girl with the Union Jack on her track suit no doubt thought she was being friendly; she did me a favour in a funny sort of way.

'Oh you must be Alex Archer from New Zealand!' she said, matching up my black togs to my New Zealand bag as we both began to strip off. 'The only swimmer. You're supposed to be quite good, aren't you!' She must have read the same magazine as her lecherous team-mate Matthew. She was in the same events as me; I'd vaguely heard of her, as a 63-plus sprinter. She'd had a good season, swum in international meetings in

England and Europe. This was her first Olympics and her whole family had come to Rome too. She came from Cambridge, that's the university town (I *know* that), and she had an uncle and aunt who went to New Zealand about five years ago, to a rather grim little place somewhere, called Hamilton. About eighty miles south of Auckland, I said. 'They emigrated, but really they said it was like England in the 1930s. No culture, you know, theatre or concerts, no proper pubs, nothing to do at weekends. They came back.'

By then I'd realized two things had happened — she'd asked nothing about me, and she'd been rude about my country, and it wasn't even psychological warfare, she didn't even know she was doing it! I listened smiling as she prattled on in her high ra-ra voice, complaining about the ghastly Italian heat, hard beds, and oily food.

'My aunt couldn't get over the food in New Zealand.' Oh? I said. 'Well, you send over all that lamb and butter, but she said the restaurants were terrible, you couldn't have wine with your meals and there were no fish-shops to speak of. And the natives ate nothing but hogget.' I smiled back, thinking *we call people like your aunt whingeing poms.* By the time she left, friendly to the last 'Ciao, Alex, see you heats Friday,' I knew I was a colonial and not really to be taken seriously. When I see you heats Friday, Miss Britain 1960, don't expect me to smile again. There was only one answer to Brits who saw me as colonial and Aussies who saw me as a little sister, if they saw me at all, and that was to forget the whole lot of them. Get on with it, do what I had to do, as well as I could, alone.

Wednesday night a sort of hush hung over the village. People lingered over the evening meal before going off to press their uniforms or write letters before early bed. The juke-box I heard in the distance from my window most nights was silent. Even the traffic seemed to be grow quiet earlier.

'Hey, kiddo, when you going to turn that light out?'

The nightly nag. Zoe, while I was staring at my diary, had finished her bedtime routine of cleansers on face, cream on hands, elbows, legs, large brush rollers in her dark hair. How she

73

slept at all with those things pricking into her scalp I had no idea, but she'd snored soundly every night since we arrived.

'Ten minutes?'

She made a great show of turning away from the light, burrowing her head into the pillow to find the least painful position for sleep, which appeared to be face down on her tummy. 'Five?' She didn't even have to compete until next week! 'By the way,' she mumbled. 'What happened to our Italian friend? Haven't seen him for days.'

'Someone said he had to go back to his office, in Milan.'

'Pity,' she sighed. 'Italian men sure know how to dress. And how they look at you, wow-ie . . . I hoped . . . *please*, Alex, it's half past ten, turn it *out*.'

Her timing was terrible. I'd spent three days forgetting our Italian friend; I was frantic for sleep but here I was remembering how he'd looked at me, straight and warm, as though I *mattered*. I could have thrown something at the body under the sheet. Her enlarged head looked like a mine, in one of those British war films set in the North Sea with actors in white polo-necks being heroes. She might be the best high jumper ever produced in New Zealand *and* on her second Olympics *and* six years older than me *and* working in an office with a lovely boss who'd kept her on full pay while she was away *and* engaged to be married with a diamond ring and glory box and all but . . .

'O-*kay*,' I said, snapping my diary shut, gathering up my cotton dressing-gown, turning the light out. 'See you.'

She didn't even reply as I left the room. She probably thought I was going to the loo.

Outside, I put on my shortie dressing-gown and looked up and down the long corridor. I could hardly go downstairs looking for somewhere to write. The thought of the toilet and shower area didn't appeal; nor the laundry room which was usually locked anyway. I tiptoed up the concrete stairs to the third and top floor. The hall lights were dimmed right down. The athletes behind those doors — who were they, Dutch, Russian, Brits, Aussies, Hungarian? — were dreaming of gold medals. I'd decided to go back and sit under a light halfway down the stairs like Christopher Robin, when I saw a door marked USCITA DI SICUREZZA. Emergency exit.

Wasn't I just one big fat emergency, very much in need of fresh air? The handle turned easily. Outside was a small iron landing, with a staircase going down to the ground and a short ladder going up to the flat roof for a view of . . .

You read about people gasping at some wondrous sight, a breathtaking view. Well, it's true. I turned slowly, literally breathless. The moon, nearly full, was fabulously bright, but it was a soft pink moon with hazy edges; the moon at home is hard and white and windswept. The air felt pink and soft too, warm on my bare neck. I shut my eyes and listened. Cars still hooted, wheels squealed around a corner, a bus roared by. Horses' hooves clip-clopped, a courting couple in a fancy carriage. Italian voices, male and two female, argued somewhere below. Music, opera, a man's voice, a tenor, came quite strongly from someone's record player.

But when I opened my eyes . . . the black shapes of the village apartments, the lamps of the streets between, lights in the windows. Under the dark shadow of the Monte Mario was a ring of lights: the stadium, where tomorrow . . . the Olympic pool was just to the left, where on Friday . . .

Close to both ran the Tiber, which if I could fly like Wendy I would see below me as swift-running ancient silver. The bridge I went over every day was outlined with lamps. The moon was so bright that it caught the curved tops of the pines and the points of the cypress trees around the whole stadium area. And last, the best: along the horizon were white perfect domes rising from the straight line of the city's lights into the blackness. One much larger than the rest I imagined to be St Peter's. It was so unbelievably beautiful that I stood and laughed. Now I knew why they called it the Eternal City. Whatever happened, if I was last in my heat and/or never saw Tom Alexander again, if the Olympic Games were cancelled or if the plane crashed on the way home, I'd never forget this, the pink moon and the floodlit domes.

Hugging my knees on a concrete ledge, I thought of another moonlit vigil: sitting on the gravelly beach at Napier at one o'clock in the morning last February, gazing across the breaking white surf at the moon and an endless ocean. It was the night before another special race, the one I *had* to win against Maggie to have any chance of selection for Rome. Somehow the idea that Andy's spirit was out there somewhere in the night had made me feel strong. I'd stood my ground against a mean attempt to have me disqualified, and I'd won. It was my gift to him.

Six months later, another moon, another sleepless night, another first and last chance race. Another Alex, who wasn't proud of her memories of the past six months: bitching at my friend Julia, fighting with my family, rude at school, to a stand-in coach who rubbed me up the wrong way. Passing out legless, drunk and disorderly at a family wedding. Fighting with Andy's friend Keith, using him to damn near drown both of us. Not proud. Something kept all those people from locking me up while I trained on . . . and on . . . Without them all, I wouldn't be here.

I began to feel sleepy. It must be getting on for midnight, witching hour. Rome didn't seem a city of witches; rather one of solid Roman ghosts in battle armour, Caesar and Brutus and Cassius, the evil Caligula and Nero. Ghosts of bleeding gladiators and Christians. Ghosts in togas: men gossiping in the Forum, women cloistered inside their atrium houses. Tosca's ghost, bloody on the castle battlements, and the scheming Scarpia. It was time I went to a proper bed.

I should have thought that a fire escape would open easily from the inside, but be locked to anyone who might try to enter from the outside.

Not again. Admit it, Alex, you're a walking disaster area. Accident prone. Stuck on a rooftop the night before the Games. I peered down the fire escape but I wasn't game to try that. The security guards and dogs prowled round the wire fences of the women's quarters during the day, and logic told me that at midnight the security would be more, not less. If I got caught trying to get down, it would be the Italian carabinieri who carried guns, and total embarrassment, an international incident even, and Mr Upjohn crowing that he knew all along I'd be nothing but a nuisance in Rome.

So I kept a vigil, like knights used to keep in churches. An unavoidable vigil until morning, in what felt like a church of a sort. Strangely, I was quite calm, not cold, not unhappy. I

thought of Andy walking along the beach at Muriwai and Tom —
somewhere in Rome. I snuggled into a concrete cranny and
watched the pink moon slide across the sky. At some point in
the night the distant domes became fainter and vanished. The
few lights in the apartment blocks went out, though the traffic
never completely stopped as it did at home.

Later, when the moon was low in the sky, I woke chilled, stiff,
a bit damp. I needed to move around, to do some calisthenics.
I padded across the flat rooftop, around the circular structure
which sat in the middle. The black shadows it threw put me in
mind of temples, pillars, a courtyard, a stage: gymnasts,
drummers, musicians. Exercises turned into dance movements,
glorious stretches to the black sky. A procession, slow,
measured, solemn. Alex in a short tunic of fine linen, her long
hair plaited with gold thread, her calves braided with soft
leather, silver round her ankles and wrists, kohl around her eyes.
She moved in time to the slow drums, a stately dance requiring
perfect balance and control. Leslie Caron danced around the
fountains in *An American in Paris*, so she would dance around
a rooftop in Rome (softly mind, as a cat) in her shortie pyjamas.
Low arabesque, attitude, a beautiful port-de-bras, but no risky
jeté. Moving figures on Greek friezes, Alexandra in the lean
body of a Greek athlete, now in her tunic and now naked,
feeling the soft air on her torso, the freedom of nakedness in the
dark endless space, stretching to the stars, pulling down
strength. Alexandra watched the dance, a small part of her
laughing at the scene, at herself.

At length the procession passed. The vision faded, the dancer
dressed and sat down as the moon fell slowly behind the hills.
She slept, smiling, and when she woke the sky was at its darkest,
with just a hint of light behind the hill to the east.

Four o'clock, five? The best bet would be to climb down the
fire escape just before dawn, hoping like hell that I wasn't eaten
alive by a Dobermann. Pretend to be an athlete out for an early
run.

And that's how it worked out, when I woke again and saw the
sky turning pale lemon. I took off my dressing-gown and
wrapped it and diary into a small bundle. With top tucked into
pants, my shortie pyjamas could pass for running gear. Bare feet

— well, some runners trained in bare feet, that marathon runner Abebe Bikila from Ethiopia for one. I crept down the iron staircase, my ears peeled for guards' footsteps, dogs, any sign of life. I had to jump the last bit, a good ten feet, taking care to jump squarely and land with cushioning knees. A broken ankle would be the last straw. I jogged once around the building trying to find the main entrance.

The funny end to this tale came when I found the door locked, so I had to go around several times, and do some exercises until at last there was enough light for a runner to come down the stairway inside. I was genuinely puffed enough to fool her that I was the earliest bird. As she came out I went in. She said something incomprehensible in Swedish or Hungarian. She was short and strongly-built and probably threw something. (A couple of days later I found out it was a javelin she threw, and well enough for a medal. She recognized me in the reception area and hailed an interpreter. I had to explain that I wasn't a runner; that swimmers sometimes went for a run to relieve boredom or sore eyes — which was a load of old nonsense. Like most swimmers I couldn't run to save myself, and I'd never given in to the pain of sore eyes in that terrible pool at home.) I jogged up the stairs to the second floor, heady with relief. The door opened without a squeak. My alarm clock said ten to six. Zoe didn't stir as I wiped off my sweaty brow and armpits with a towel, climbed into bed and started, silently, to laugh.

Nessun dorma

Two days into my self-imposed banishment — I've been unexpectedly lonely. Something's missing. So I've been, despite the incredible heat, walking; through the Trastevere, the Borghese gardens, yesterday out at Tivoli, through Hadrian's villa, the Villa d'Este, the Canopus valley. All wonderful . . . yet I keep thinking of a certain pool where the swimmers, surely the only people in Rome comfortable in this heat, have been having their last training sessions before the historic ceremony tomorrow and the swimming events the day after. Alex's first race, her début. I'm sure it will not be her last and only one.

I have just come home, on the eve of the opening ceremony, exhausted, having walked from the Campidoglio. Maybe three miles, though it felt like six. It's 2.00 a.m. The apartment bedroom, though large and with the ceiling fan going, still feels airless and is probably well over 90°F. With sleep eluding me, I have got up and sung through some gentle Schubert pieces, some Cole Porter, played some Bach preludes, some two-part inventions, some Debussy, Chopin nocturnes, the slow movements of two Mozart sonatas, Schumann's little Kinderszenen, to little avail.

I'd be surprised if Alex, or indeed any of the athletes, can sleep tonight. *Nessun dorma.* Turandot, Pekingese version, has been so comatose in her basket that I have several times in the past few days thought she had died. I understand the quarters in the village are not air-conditioned. I hope her room is fitted with a fan.

I had not intended to go to the Campidoglio, but the crowds seemed to be gathering in that direction and for want of any other commitment, I went with them. Soon after dark I understood why. With operatic pomp, all sorts of dignitaries and uniforms were assembled, lamps were lit, bands played, the equestrian statue of Marcus Aurelius and the encircling statues splendidly floodlit; something Italy does as well as any country. Eventually a lone runner came springing up the steps carrying aloft the Olympic flame, from, I understand, Olympia, via the Peloponnese, Athens, Sicily, and up through Italy, carried by a multitude of young runners. I wish Alex had been here, to share it — especially when the boy prodded his torch into the waiting bowl and lit the leaping orange flame; ancient Olympia come to Michelangelo's Rome, too much for a humble Kiwi. I think she would have shared my tears.

From the balcony I can see the moon, rosy and soft-edged, unlike a New Zealand full moon which I remember to be a hard dead white. *Nessun dorma.*

A long march

Alex, you've been here before!

It wasn't just the rehearsal, when we'd marched past the silent empty stands. There was something weirdly familiar as we went into the tunnel. Into the blessed shade, and the image clicked: the procession at ancient Olympia, going into the arena as one of the athletes would have seen it: inside a square tunnel with the parade walking ahead, some naked, others wearing armour and carrying spears; and ahead, the first glimpse of crowd waiting in the stadium. I could see, sharp as a photograph, the page in my classical history book, the caption under the artist's impression: "The parade of athletes assembled in the courtyard in front of the Temple of Zeus and then marched through a narrow tunnel into the adjacent stadium."

'This is it folks,' said a voice behind, male trying hard to be unimpressed, laconic. 'The light at the end of the . . .'

'Shut up, Gary, you silly bastard,' said others. This tunnel was much bigger than the one in the picture, and *we* all had clothes on (far too many, near-dead after two miles in high heels) but surely those Greek athletes had felt just like me, swept along, faces wet with sweat, hardly breathing, numb with excitement. Our footsteps echoed left-right left-right off the sides as we marched towards the light and the sound of the bands and that vast roaring crowd we knew was in there.

It must be about four o'clock. By rights, I shouldn't still be standing. From my night under the pink moon to no more sleep, tiny breakfast, loosening-up swim only before a tiny lunch. Put on uniform, assemble with teams, blazers of every colour under the sun, flag-bearers, placard-bearers out on the roads around the village, interminable wait, buy drinks, more drinks in the blinding heat, but not so many that we'd need to pee. There'd be no comfort stop, once we got going. Curse the people who put us in thick black blazers and high heels. Finally move off, march down riverside road (I was stiff from my dawn jog, tomorrow will be worse, *tomorrow* — aaargh — I have to swim), through the Ponte Milvio over the Tiber with helicopter above, through the Stadio dei Marmi with its huge white statues peering down and stands full of people, cheers, crowds, music, bunting, flags — this was what we came for.

And then we were through the tunnel and the sunlight hit us again, and the first sight and noise of a hundred thousand people, surrounded by a gigantic sweep of faces, and I felt, for the first time, yes, we *are* special, me and my mates marching around this red track behind our flag, we're athletes, and the best. All you people have come to honour us, honour the spirit of the Games, just as they used to at Olympia.

I wondered where the press box was. Up behind the V.I.P. stand, no doubt.

Burning a ring around my wrist, contrary to a silly rule which said no jewellery with uniform, was a new silver charm bracelet. It had been mysteriously delivered that morning, by special messenger. A black velvet box wrapped in shiny pink paper. Inside, on grey satin, was the bracelet, with a single charm. A musical symbol, a bass clef holding together five lines, the music stave. His signature. Zoe and some of the others had bought charm bracelets in Singapore. They were clunky; this was very classy-looking, with an Italian name from Firenze inside the lid. There was no card, and no need for one. Baritones use the bass clef. He'd asssumed I knew that. I hadn't told him I learnt music.

If you're up in the press box, I thought, as we marched down the long straight track in front of the main stand, I'm the young one in the second row, with the taller women, second from the right. You might be able to see a glint of silver round my right wrist. I'm not going to turn my head, because this is eyes-front left-right stuff, and I am, as you said at lunch last Sunday, a professional in attitude if not hard cash. I am Alexandra, at the Olympic Games! I made it!

Around the red curve of the track, we heard special cheers from Kiwis up in the stands. Behind us the noise surged, loud for the huge U.S.A. team, loudest of all for Italy as the host, in sky-blue blazers. From the grassy centre of the stadium, lined up with the other teams, I could now pick out the V.I.P. stand facing us and yes, the press box with rows of desks. Behind us, the bowl stood on the skyline, where the runner would light the flame. Under the scoreboard, bands, orchestras, choirs. Around me people took photos and let off steam about the size of the crowd, the heat and sun, the people back home who chose our uniform, sore feet. The runners rejoiced they didn't have to compete for a week, forgetting that some did. I'd have given *anything* to sit down. One clever man, a yachtsman, produced one of those folding seats on a walking stick, and perched on it, grinning smugly.

They trumpeted the V.I.P.s in for speeches in Italian and English. Eight sailors in white sailor-suits escorted in the Olympic flag. They handed over the flag from the last Olympics in Melbourne. They fired off the loudest cannons I'd ever heard in my life, and let loose about nine million pigeons. Everyone ducked, but no one actually got bombed before they headed off to the hills. The sun dropped below the rim of the stadium, giving us shade.

The arrival of the Olympic torch finished me off. The announcer said something in Italian. There was a complete hush apart from distant cheers outside the stadium, and then we heard the cry swell from those near the entrance. We'd been told not to break rank on pain of death, but how could you not; everyone did spontaneously, officials and all. We just *had* to see. I got only a glimpse of the dark boy in white running shorts, the torch held high. The noise, already incredible, got louder and louder as he ran past the athletes jammed around the inside of the track and up the steps towards the skyline. He paused while the crowd roared, then plunged the torch into the bowl. The flame burst upwards. I wasn't the only one with a wet face as we were herded back into line. Someone who knew said the boy was the Roman secondary school athletics champion.

The rest — the flags being paraded, and an Italian competitor taking the oath on behalf of all the athletes, the Italian national anthem, all seemed a bit of an anti-climax. Then we were on the move again, marching out, taking the short way back to the village.

The other women chose to amble and buy drinks and talk to people from other teams, but I told Bulldog that I was going on ahead. She was too tired to argue and I kept going like a robot, because I had to swim tomorrow and if I didn't take off my blazer (against regulations) and keep walking, I'd fall over or seize up completely. My dawn jog was the maddest thing I'd ever done. The Aussies and Canadians, being among the first out, would have been the first back to their quiet rooms. To think about Tomorrow.

Halfway across the bridge the white concrete started to go blurry and black around the edges. I was going to pass out. We'd been told that blazers were to stay on, all day. The thought of an ambulance was worse than being told off. I pulled my shirt out of my tight skirt and hung gasping for air, my mouth dry as sand, over the rail. Slowly the river scene in front of me came back into focus. The Tiber surged around the piles of the bridge, white swirls in dark turquoise. I could see the tops of the pool stands. My stomach lurched.

I thought of another bridge: the Auckland harbour bridge being opened last year and Andy and I walking with the crowds. He'd quoted Kipling at me and we'd talked of death, whether you'd live if you fell off. This bridge was not nearly as high. Fifteen months, was that all? Andy was dead, and I was here.

A small thanks-offering was required, to him, to Rome. I slowly undid the chain of his only gift to me, the pearl tear-drop I always wore. I didn't hesitate, just let it gently drop into the turquoise. It flashed milky-white once, his tear, my tears. Perhaps it would be carried to the sea, or stay in the mud on the riverbed. Quite fitting for a pearl.

I walked the last half mile back to the village in a daze through the crowds of ambling athletes, and the last bit through the village in my stockings because my feet felt as though they had been amputated. I staggered up the last stairs. The room was absolutely suffocating. It was about 6.30 p.m. Throw open the shutters. Take off all clothes! Bed! Horizontal! I hadn't sat down for seven hours! Tomorrow!

'Telephone!'

It was, of course, only a bad dream.

'Telephone, wake up. For you, Alex. From New Zealand, quick.'

'Go away.'

'From home, Godzone . . . cripes, Alex, home, *New Zealand*,' someone yelled in my ear. 'Gee, what a gorgeous bracelet, where did you get it!'

'Mind your own . . .' The words slipped sideways out of my mouth as I slid back into the void.

'Listen, it's the *telephone*.'

'So what.'

'Telephone, for you, person-to-person, long-distance. Someone called Mrs Young is spending good money to talk to you, God knows why.'

'It's probably my Gran,' I said loftily, 'rung to wish me luck.' My eyes would not open. 'It *is* my Gran.' I staggered onto the floor. 'Where? Lead me.'

'Put something on, for God's sake.' Zoe found my dressing-gown. 'If you went to bed earlier . . .'

'Nag, nag.' I vaguely knew the phone was downstairs, and that I needed Zoe's help to get there. She pushed me stumbling out the door, and led me down the stairs. It seemed to be night-time.

'Hullo?' A voice asked me if I was Miss Alexandra Archer, then I heard . . . Gran, sounding like she was round the back of the moon. 'How are you, my pet?'

'What time's it there, Gran?'

'Never mind the time. Tell me about . . . we were listening on the wireless, on shortwave.'

'You sound all blurry. It's an awful line.'

'Tell me, pet.'

'It was amazing, incredible. I cried when we marched around, I felt so proud. When the boy lit the flame I thought I'd die. Rome's *hot*.' I suddenly felt dirty and completely disoriented. 'What's the time there, Gran?'

'We just, on the midday news.' She sounded a bit breathless. 'They said the New Zealand team looked very smart, and marched beautifully. I wanted to say good luck for your race. God bless you always, Alex.'

There was a slight pause, then I heard Mum's voice, and Dad's in the background. No one said anything special, really, except hullo, how are you feeling, fighting fit I hope, had your bottom pinched (Dad) and how's your Italian (Mum), how's everyone at home, we're fine, the kids send their love, they're at school, of course, Mr Jack sends his love, good luck and gofurrit, bye Alex, swim well, thinking of you, love you.

The line went static, the thread broken. I wished they hadn't rung, because I stood in that dim empty hallway, not knowing what time of the day or night it was, gone from thrill to misery. Zoe took the phone out of my hand and silently pushed me up the stairs. My travel clock said quarter to eleven, apparently night-time.

'Odd time to ring,' said Zoe, taking off clothes, not her uniform.

'Where've you been? Weren't you in bed?'

'I was just coming up the stairs when the phone rang. Bit of a party developed in one of the recreation areas — dancing to the juke-box, doing the conga. All *sorts* were there, Americans, Africans, Japanese, Aussies.'

Only high-jumpers and the like, I thought sourly, who still have a week before their events. Not swimmers who'd all be stiff after the march and desperately trying to sleep. 'At least it didn't wake you up,' I said, pointedly.

'No, but they woke you, from the dead. I'd have thought, the night before your big race . . .'

'Probably they didn't want to miss me tomorrow, knowing I'd be coming and going to the pool. They know I'm a good sleeper,' I lied. By the time I'd washed away the day's sweat and grime in the shower, I'd nearly convinced myself that this was true, that the timing wasn't a bit peculiar. It was a long and desperate night that I had to get through.

Overture

Since I can't sleep again, I must sing or write.

The music, I thought, was the least impressive feature of the opening ceremony this afternoon. For a nation passionately devoted to music of the dramatic ceremonial kind, it was distant and uninspiring. The British do these things better.

As spectacle, though, true to Baron de Coubertin's prescribed format, it was breathtaking. I had, from the press box dead centre of the main stand, a ringside seat! I arrived early, because it had occurred to me, jolting awake at 4.00 a.m., that Norm Thompson didn't actually know that he and his paper had acquired me as his personal interpreter/copy assistant. He was, as I hoped, in the face of a certain amount of disarming honesty, more amused than put out. The man looks seedy — he says he is not coping well with the heat, or his hotel food. I felt only slightly an opportunist.

Or perhaps he understood the deeper reason. When the New Zealand team marched through the tunnel into the arena, their black-and-white colour scheme smarter among the many-coloured uniforms than I might have expected, he silently handed me his binoculars for a brief look. I haven't seen her for four days. I picked her immediately in the second row, the tallest woman, walking distinctively and superbly erect. Even from that distance her eyes burned; a sort of solemn 'I don't believe this is happening to me' incredulity.

Above his retrieved binoculars, Norm gave me a running commentary as the team passed below us. He'd covered three Olympiads and five Empire Games, he said, but the parades always churned him up. He knew most of the athletes pretty well — Alex when she first started swimming lessons, a small, determined kid aged eight or nine. Her coach saw her potential, even then. That dark horse Peter Snell too, a promising tennis player before he took to pounding round that lethal circuit of Arthur Lydiard's out at Titirangi.

To my question: what chance did Alex have tomorrow? he replied that it was impossible to say. She was fitter, and tougher, than she herself thought, but she'd not raced since April. She could go either way — sink without trace, or rise to the occasion. Today's long march wouldn't help.

I enjoyed watching the world's top sports reporters working at their microphones and Olivettis, two-finger typists many of them. Norm wrote his copy as the ceremony proceeded and I was able to earn my keep, securing a long-distance line for him back to Auckland. I lost all sight of Alex, despite the binoculars, when the athletes broke ranks to see the torch-bearer do his triumphal circuit. I thought I might have glimpsed her among the teams as they returned to the village, but I was defeated by the crowds; and I have made a promise.

As dusk fell, I slowly rode the Vespa, borrowed this morning, alongside the river. The apartment is mercifully cool and solitary. I'll not watch any of the television coverage; I've seen the ceremony, I have a treasured memory, I don't need the facsimile.

Today, though magnificent, was merely the overture; tomorrow is the first act. I wonder how she is sleeping, if at all. One day I'll face the same ordeal, the night before a début in a small role in — where? a major house in Rome or Milan or London, or more realistically, some small repertory theatre in Germany? — knowing that I have done everything in my power to prepare myself, and can humanly do no more.

Those burning blue-grey eyes do not tell of failure and are beginning, as I sing through some Schumann, to haunt me.

A ruddy miracle

So, it's actually going to happen. You're going to stand on the block in front of twenty thousand people for the race you've dreamed of for five years.

It'll be a ruddy miracle if I get into the semi-finals tomorrow. I didn't sleep a wink. My calves were sore from all the walking. I felt sick over breakfast, got mad at Mrs C and madder at Mr Upjohn both wanting to organize me. I had diarrhoea. All that brave talk about adjusting body-clocks for a mid-afternoon race went out the window. I couldn't face either food or rugby talk at lunch. Bulldog brought me a doggy bag, I gnawed on a bread roll. I shaved my arms and legs, and checked my gear seventeen times over. Mr Upjohn brought me a huge pile of telegrams from home, which merely made me weep. He gave me a sealed envelope from Mr Jack. 'Go out hard, but leave something for the run home, 110 per cent effort in the final 25 yards. Remember Napier, you did it then. Remember you start as equals. Good luck, Enjoy it. Ta-Ta For Now. Your cuddly friend, Bill Jack.' *Enjoy* it?

A second parcel arrived, smaller. Inside was a black velvet box from the same jeweller. A tiny silver kiwi sat on grey satin. Did you have it specially made, Tom? Firenze jewellers wouldn't even know what a kiwibird was, or why. I clipped it carefully into the silver strands of the bracelet. Two charms, two messages around my wrist. You are a Kiwi, you have a friend here, don't forget it.

To the pool at one-thirty, half a bread roll sticking in my gullet, calves still stiff. Warm-up in the covered pool with the naked horse murals felt like I was swimming in treacle. No one talked much in the changing-room. Even Dawn Fraser looked tired and grim in her corner, and she was supposed to be an old hand at this. Which would be worse being defending Olympic champ or a scared shitless first-timer?

Ten to three. Thirty grim females from eighteen countries in the marshalling area, a large bare room near the changing-rooms. We had wet hair from our warm-up, and track suits with Union Jacks, or Stars 'n Stripes, maple leaves, Aussie maps, lots of different flags. Miss Britain 1960, for all her earlier aplomb, was positively grey around the gills. Some looked like grannies in old-fashioned towelling dressing-gowns. It was just like home really. Same elderly officials with clipboards, same wrinkly chaperones clucking about, same restless bodies, same fear.

They called the first heat, la prima batteria. Being in the last, at least I could get some idea of the times. They filed out five or six zombies at a time, 25 left, then 19, 12, then six. I counted. We could tell exactly what was happening by the crowd noises filtering in through the open door — four times over, the names being announced, claps and cheers, the hush, the gun, the rising roar of the race, the climax, the results, applause. Dawn Fraser won the second heat, 62.1. Cripes! First and third heats, over 64s, encouraging. Chris Von Saltza the fourth, in Olympic record time of 61.9. Double cripes!

The last six, a Brit, East Germans, Canadian. Me, lane 6, good for me; on the return lap the field would be on my breathing side. So I was the last female to walk, towel around my neck, through the dim tunnel into . . .

Such *blinding* light that I couldn't see anything for about a minute. Tom, you up there, I don't want to see either. I kept my eyes on the heels of the girl in front, all the way up the long side of the pool staring at the pink paving until I realized she had stopped at lane 5. I had to move on to lane 6. When I looked up, I very nearly ran pronto for the tunnel.

I knew the pool well enough with empty stands. Full was another matter. This was what 20,000 people looked like, buzzing with excitement 'cause they'd just seen an Olympic record. The sunlight was coming onto the pool twice over from the white sky and reflected from the white crowd. The pool looked like a shimmering transparent turquoise stage.

Blinking, my heart g-donking away, I tried to think straight. Around the starting area were about four hundred officials in grey blazers and panama hats, the judges in tiers above the finish. At the far end, the scoreboard showed 4ª Batteria, ranging from Chris Von Saltza's 61.9 to someone who'd done 69.0. Well I could beat 69 with my legs tied! What I had to beat was 64. Swim faster than I'd ever swum. It wasn't possible. If I walked away now, if I swam a 66s, people would understand. I was still only fifteen.

I deliberately did not look up towards the press box, above the starting blocks. I knew I could probably pick out a flashy hat, a pink shirt. I knew he was there. I would not look. I was here to swim, not to flirt, and swim I would, damn you. I am Alex the pro, getting on with the job. Thank you for the silver kiwi.

Finally, introduced to the crowd — Signorina Alessandra Archer, dalla Nuova Zelanda — stripped to racers, smoothed limbs, bareheaded or in caps, we stood on the steps of our blocks. As I drew in lungfuls of air, I thought of Maggie, our show-down race in Napier. I had five Maggies to beat this time.

You've not seen me *really* in action yet, Tom, my Kiwi friend, you with the hat on.

A whistle, a hush. *Al posto!* The crouching wait, toes curled, feet ready to thrust, knees to straighten, arms to fling. No one is trying to break. I'm feeling steady. Finally, my Olympic gun.

It was my first proper race for five months. I didn't deserve it. It was one of those few races where everything went right. A great start, felt smooth, rhythmic, easy. Keeping up, from what I could see of the bodies under the water to my right. Turn perfectly timed, push-off strong.

Now I could see the opposition. Still keeping up. Still double-breathing comfortably. *Still* keeping up? Look again, Alex. Bloody hell!

Halfway up the return length I saw only one head was actually level, the others were behind. I had a chance. The time might be okay too. I gave it everything I had.

Above me the timekeepers drew back, the noise of the vast crowd fell over me like a breaking wave. I flopped back into a

91

slow-motion backstroke. They were using special stopwatches started by the gun and stopped by the timekeepers; the first time at a Games.

The list flashed up:

1 STEWARD, G.B.   63.5
2 ARCHER, N.Z.   63.8
3 . . .

I shook the water from my eyes.

2 ARCHER — I turned and did a dolphin dive. When I came up it was still there. ARCHER, N.Z. 63.8.

It wasn't possible. I've never swum faster. Tom, my friend up there, did you *see* me? I think I might have qualified.

'You've qualified,' said Mrs C, glowing all over with disbelief.

'You've qualified,' said Mr Upjohn, even more incredulous. 'Well done, child,' they chorused as I found my way back to the changing-room.

'*You've* qualified,' said Miss Britain 1960 with the voice like the Queen and the aunt who hated New Zealand. It turned out she was the seventeenth fastest, in a time one second off her best, of course in the *toughest* heat. So she'd just missed out on the semi-final. I was the thirteenth fastest, she informed me, with just the slightest hint that somehow it was all wrong, that I'd upset the natural balance of things.

Not bad, I thought, towelling my hair dry, for a colonial hick. 'Sorry, Sheila,' I said in the broadest New Zealand accent I could muster. 'That's not my name,' she said. 'Oh, but it is,' I said. 'All girls are Sheila in New Zealand. Didn't your aunt tell you, of course she wasn't really there long enough to find out, was she?' I gathered up my bags. She didn't know what I was talking about. 'Ciao, Sheila.' I don't like being patronized.

'You're through, kiddo,' said Dawn Fraser, clapping me on the shoulder as I sidled past her in the corridor. 'Good swim, Alex Archer.' She knew I existed, my *name*? I wondered if she could see my whole body going red as I mumbled 'Thanks. Great swim of yours, too,' and fled.

'You're in, Kiwi' said a delighted Norm Thompson waiting for me outside the pool, with Mr U and Mrs C. 'I might have known you wouldn't be satisfied, coming all this way for one race.'

'No comment,' I grinned.

'I've a message,' he said, while Mr Upjohn was diverted by a passing Australian official. 'From a certain I-tie journo who was watching the race with me. He sends, let's see — he made me write it down.' He found an entry in amongst a page of untidy shorthand notes. 'Saluti auguri e congratulazioni!'

'No comment,' I grinned again. I was wearing the bass clef and the silver kiwi on my wrist.

My British friend was right in one thing: the balance *had* been altered. At dinner that night some of the New Zealand men who'd not said two words to me since we left home suddenly came out with 'Great stuff, girlie', and 'You beaudy', and the like.

Telegrams — FANTASTIC, KEEP IT UP, BEST LUCK FOR SATURDAY — poured in, much better than GOOD TRY or more likely nothing at all, had I failed the first post. Mr Upjohn was conspicuous by his presence and rather politer than before. New Zealand didn't have too much to crow about at Olympic swimming level. Jean Stewart won a backstroke bronze in Helsinki '52 and Marrion Roe, who was a senior when I was just starting, reached the sprint finals in Melbourne four years ago. Could I pull it off again? 'A possible finalist', a British magazine writer had said.

Instead of filing remarks like 'Fifteen-year-old Alex Archer swam gamely in her heat but was outclassed', Norm Thompson was now writing back things like 'Fifteen-year-old Alex Archer rose splendidly to the challenge with a heat time equalling her best. The achievement of this, coming from winter training and suffering from mild dysentery and sunburn in Rome's 104°F afternoon heat, cannot be underestimated.'

I didn't know that at the time, of course, only later when I saw Mum's scrap book. But I'd jumped out of the frying pan into the fire. I could hardly force two mouthfuls down my throat at dinner, and the small print of the paperback edition of *War and Peace* I was trying to read kept blurring before my eyes. Zoe didn't even nag me to turn out the light. I must have slept, because I dreamed a Hollywood production number, me in ridiculous white gloves in a water ballet one minute and swimming a race the next, while around the pool marched an army of identical young men with lurid red hair carrying flaming torches. The Colosseum came in somewhere, too, like that film *Quo Vadis*, lions and blood, the bloodthirsty crowd . . . Around five I woke for about the tenth time, sweating.

I wondered what the dawn looked like from the roof, my special sanctuary. This time I took a sandal for the emergency door, to make sure it stayed open. This was about as silent as Rome ever got — an occasional car, a set of faint church bells on one note, roosters, a baby crying. I hadn't sat long in the cool hush before the black domes appeared against grey, lemon, pink, orange, and finally crimson streaked with black.

I spent the next three dawns on the roof, soaking up a sky so beautiful I sat in tears, telling myself that it was all worth it. I could have been the seventeenth fastest and saved myself some of the agony.

You've left behind country, family, friends, your coach. Mr Upjohn greases and Bulldog fusses, and you're indifferent. The telegrams are nice, but they don't touch you — you have trouble remembering who half the people are. When you left home you knew trouble was brewing in the Congo. Now World War III could have started somewhere for all you knew. You hadn't heard any proper news for two weeks. You don't hear the gossip and you don't look at anyone in the changing room. They thought you were a snotty bitch.

I felt aged eleven again, and on my own. Completely and utterly.

The one person who mattered, I'd let walk out of my life without a protest. Saturday lunchtime another charm arrived in a black velvet box, this time a silver fern like the emblem on our blazer pockets. I come from New Zealand. I am swimming for my country. He is still around somewhere. I will not look up at the press box.

The semi-finals were scheduled for 8.40 Saturday night. I dragged myself through the morning swim, re-ran the endless suffocating hours between token lunch, tossing siesta, reading without seeing, token tea, the deliberately slow showering/

94

shaving ritual, not because I needed to, but because it was something to *do*.

In the bus to the pool Mr Upjohn gave me another sealed letter from Mr Jack. *ALEX ARCHER (N.Z.)* — *100m SEMI-FINALIST* it said on the outside. *To be opened on Saturday, August 27.* Oh Mr Jack, you believed! I read it in the toilet, through tears. I could almost hear his cuddly Aussie voice, telling me that I *can* win a place in the final, I have done the work, I proved yesterday I have the speed, I must give this one everything I had, go out fast, and stay out.

By 8.30 the world's sixteen fastest female swimmers, representing ten nations, were pacing around the call area. You could have cut the air with a knife. At 8.45 the first eight filed out, heads down. I'd drawn lane 2 in the second semi-final, a disaster for me because on the return run I wouldn't see a thing. I'd be swimming blind. Dawn Fraser was in lane 4. She had big rings under her eyes. She didn't talk to me or anyone.

We stood in line, one to eight, began to walk towards the tunnel. I saw the pool spread out in front of me, the water dramatically blue under the strongest floodlights I've ever seen in my life. Yellow lane ropes, red flags, pink concourse, white officials' trousers. Unreal colours, like a very clear dream. The stands soared upwards into the black. I heard the girl behind me muttering to herself as we began that long lonely walk up the length of the pool, walking the plank to watery doom. Maybe she was a Catholic, praying.

Tom, I'm the one in the black track suit, second in the line, with inadequate wobbly legs like the Scarecrow in *The Wizard of Oz*. I was the Scarecrow once, not so long ago, with a silver face. I made a great fool of myself. I'm about to do it again.

We were introduced (this time I registered some New Zealand cheers from the stands) and again faced the scoreboard. 1ª Semi-finale. 1 C. VON SALTZA, U.S.A. 62.5. The slowest time was 65.6, the cut-off point at fourth was 64.7. Mine could be the faster heat. It had to be under 64 for me to have any chance at all.

Well, I thought, this might be the first and last time I ever swim against Dawn Fraser, so I might as well make the most of it. She looked reluctant to move to the blocks.

I was just about to take my track suit top off when I realized I still had Tom's charm bracelet on. I couldn't get it undone. Then it got hooked up in my track suit sleeve. A woman official came to my aid, but by this time I was just slightly keeping them all waiting, and bright scarlet. If Tom had binoculars, he'd have seen why. Okay, I thought angrily, glowing like a Christmas tree, my nerve ends jangling like bells, watch me, matey.

What did I expect, really? This little pipsqueak upstart aged fifteen from the colonies? Halfway up the first length I could see Dawn Fraser, two lanes away, already slightly ahead, going like the proverbial Bondi tram. I felt tight, no rhythm. I might have been third or fourth to the turn. That, at least, wasn't too bad.

The trip home was one of those endless nightmares, blinded by lights, fighting the water, buffeted by the wash, swallowing water. But I sure as hell wasn't going to throw it away. I tried to ride up on my bow-wave. I really did try for you, Mr Jack, heart, soul, and every bit of puff I had. My arms hurt, my legs hurt, my chest hurt and I had no idea where anyone else was. When I touched and looked across, I knew at least I wasn't last.

A great cheer went up. FRASER (AUST) 61.4, new Olympic record. Flash bulbs were going off all over the place. Then the other names came up on the board.

ORDINE DI ARRIVO: 1 FRASER (AUST)   61.4
                      2 ARCHER (N.Z.)   63.5

What? This time I followed Dawn Fraser and went for a long wind-down swim, feeling the pain seep out of my muscles, telling myself I was seeing things, cruel tricks of the night. They'd got it all wrong. They'd announce a correction, the new system had broken down. Ladies and Gentlemen . . . there has been a terrible mistake. Or whatever it was in Italian.

When I could bring myself to look again, halfway up the pool and that much closer, my name was still there, large as life, and second down. ARCHER 63.5. Personal best ever. After such an excruciating race, I don't believe it. Dawn Fraser looked across at me as we both hauled ourselves out together, and grinned and nodded. She'd just set an Olympic record, but she knew I'd come second. So it must be true.

I think I am an Olympic finalist.

Everything changed again.

So recently ignored, how do you now cope finding yourself being congratulated by people who should by rights have been in the final? The champs of Britain, Hungary, Italy, Sweden, Germany, Canada? Some could shake your hand and smile, ruefully, with eyes that said where the hell did you pop up from? Others wouldn't even look but turned away, their whole bodies drooping with despair. All that work . . . you knew the feeling.

You didn't cope well at all. There was too much emotion charging around. You started to shake uncontrollably and escaped to the toilet to throw up what little food was in your stomach. You dressed in there too, numbed, fumbling in your haste to escape. You had a moment of panic when you couldn't remember where your charm bracelet had gone. You found it in your track suit pocket. You'd nearly swum the jolly race with it on!

Out of the changing-room, you got no further than Mr Upjohn and a group of ancient reporters, several from home, including Norm Thompson, four Aussies. You got confused, you answered their stupid questions like a dumb twelve-year-old, you bored them, you bored yourself. How many brothers and sisters, Miss Archer? Boyfriends, Miss Archer? Do you know what do you want to be, Miss Archer? Three, no and no.

You longed to see someone you knew under the age of sixty, preferably male, 23, and red-haired. You were on the verge of asking Norm Thompson if you could come up to the press box, when he gave you a note with a single word: *Bravissima!* You stood, tingling, poised, in the middle of the entrance hall with the naked bronze statues. You heard Bulldog say 'Alex, what do you want to do?' You walked out, down the steps. He could wait, you could wait.

You sleepwalked through two days of dreamy white heat. You saw the dawn and the sunrise and heard church bells on Sunday. You stacked the telegrams around your dressing-table mirror. You went late to meals, to avoid your team-mates' teasing, and their endless post-mortems about the All Blacks losing the fourth test and the series to the South Africans who sat crowing loudly at the other end of the dining hall. You went 'training'. You 'slept', dozed, looked at the ceiling, stood under cold showers for half an hour at a time. You 'read' *War and Peace.*

You still couldn't believe it. Even if you only came eighth, you'd always be 'an Olympic finalist'. Did Tom, who knew nothing about sport, work that out too? His Sunday message came via Norm Thompson at the pool. It was the Olympic symbol, five interlocking rings, in silver and enamel, barely half an inch across. You put it on the bracelet. You could wait.

Monday's message was unmistakable: a tiny medal with a wreath around the edges. Engraved on one side was *La Grande Olimpiade, Roma, 1960,* and on the other, *Sig. Alex Archer, New Zealand.* The point was, it was bronze.

At first, you were angry. What did he know about it? It was obvious that the battle for the gold would be between Dawn Fraser and Chris Von Saltza. But third, bronze? Did he, anyone, really expect you to beat all those seasoned Europeans into third, the bronze?

You dreamed. You had already, God knows how, lowered your own personal best twice. Could you pull it off a third time? Perhaps, a 63.0 might just do it? It was unlikely. It was possible. Okay, Tom, it was *possible.*

At Monday lunchtime, you took two calls, person-to-person from home — Mum only, on behalf of the family, and Mr Jack. There was a conspiracy going on. 'The bronze?' she said. 'The bronze,' he said. You laughed. It was one o'clock in the morning over there. They must have been on the plonk together. You had nine hours to go.

Your body refused to sleep or take food. You shaved it, showered it, prepared its bag, read its telegrams once more to give you some Dutch courage because you had none of the real sort, and finally you walked it out of your room to meet a stranger in a blazer called Mrs Churchill; out of the women's quarters, over to the main entrance to catch the bus to the pool. Your race was at nine. You still had three hours to go.

You walked past the bronze statues — why was everybody obsessed with bronze? — down to the silent changing-rooms. You had a 'warm-up' under the murals, in the pool made of marble. Your arms felt like they were attached to someone else. You wished, again, passionately, that you'd been the seventeenth fastest and saved yourself three days of agony.

In the toilet you read Mr Jack's final message to *ALEX ARCHER, FINALIST,* which reduced you to a sobbing mess. He'd thought even then that you could get this far? *This time, Alex, you must swim the race of your life. T.T.F.N.*

You endured half an hour in the call area. Dawn Fraser looked even more miserable. Chris Von Saltza, now that you were seeing her up close, was very blonde, Scandinavian-looking. You were called in lane 7 (very good for seeing on the return lap, for what it was worth), and you walked seventh into the strong light, beginning that march up the side of the pool for a race you never in your wildest dreams thought you'd swim.

There are only two races I remember so clearly I can run them in my head like a movie, in gorgeous Technicolor with all the dialogue, crowd noises, and background music complete.

One was that night in Napier, when I knew I had to beat Maggie to have any chance of getting to Rome. I remember so clearly those dreadful false starts, the thin rope across my chest, the shocking turn, my thoughts up that despairing last lap almost as though Andy was talking to me, egging me on.

The final in Rome is the other. I remember the little procession walking up the side of the pool, eight tall strong women in track suits, towels around our necks. The roar of the crowd as we appeared, the many Aussies in the crowd already shrieking 'Go Dawnie'. I remember the dozens of officials in their grey blazers, the tier of judges, the yellow lane-ropes, the sheen of the water, the floodlights shining down onto the pool from the very top of those vast stands.

Being introduced: *Cento metri stile libero, donne . . . dalla Nuova Zelanda, numero sette, la signorina Alessandra Archer,* with the rolled rrrs, and smiling at not a bad clap from all those people for the youngest competitor in the race. Smiling in the direction, way up the top, of some special cheers and yells, the sort you hear around rugby fields: 'Go, Kiwi.'

I remember looking up at the scoreboard at the other end, my name unbelievably there, lane 7, and thinking: let's see how high I notch it up the Ordine di Arrivo, to five, to four, to . . . I remember looking across at Dawn Fraser, standing quite still, hunched, her fingertips quivering, and knowing just from the murderous way she was staring at the water that she was going to win. I remember smiling, the very idea of beating *Dawn Fraser* is too cheeky for words, but I'm going to do better than seventh.

I remember taking a quick look up at the press box as I slowly peeled off my track suit, without seeing anyone special. But I knew he was there.

I felt tall and dangerous as I walked over to the block and stood on the first step in my black togs and stretched my arms to the black sky. I remember Bulldog's bulging eyes as she took my track suit, the lipstick on her teeth, the announcer calling for *Silenzio!* I remember those twenty thousand people falling to a rustling silence, the long whistle, someone coughing, *Al posto!* the long steady crouching silence, we are all experienced here, no one trying to get a flier, the final gun.

The race itself? The blue water and yellow lane-corks sleeking past. Feeling superb. Black sharks on my blind side. Through my bow-wave noting the girl in lane 8 already behind as we approach the turn. A perfect turn, coming out to see several heads level with mine. Only one clearly ahead.

I remember thinking, I'm dreaming, this is an Olympic final not an inter-club carnival in Auckland and I should already be knowing my place, which is to come in seventh. Instead I can see one head ahead and three others level with mine. Already only five, jostling for three medals.

Halfway home, keeping rhythm through the churning water, through the growing disbelief that still only one head is clearly ahead, or maybe two, but no more than two. I kick into my absolute top gear. A voice from the past says *Reach for a star, Alex, the one with Rome written on it.* Another says *The bronze, Alessandra.*

100

Well, it was Dawn Fraser's night, but you could say it was Down Under's night too. The undisputed champion of the world, Dawn Fraser climbed onto the victory dais, waving her koala bear to the vast cheering crowd. 'Dawnie, Dawnie, Dawnie,' they chanted. She set a new Olympic record of 61.2, and became the first swimmer ever to retain an Olympic crown.

I touched the wall, and died. When I looked across, Chris Von Saltza was already hanging over the lane ropes, congratulating Dawn Fraser. Other heads came raggedly home. The timekeepers above me had pulled back. I couldn't look at the board. I went for a swim. Twenty yards up the pool I turned and came back. I still couldn't look.

Then I heard a very penetrating voice from not very far away that didn't carry above the crowd noise but somehow came underneath it. 'Bravissima, bellissima, Alessandra.'

Bravissima for what, Tom, oh bronze man? Fifth? Even fourth? FRASER, VON SALTZA . . . I knew the board didn't lie, and there were no tricks.

3 A. ARCHER (N.Z.) 63.0. I was third?

I'd won the bronze?

He was right there on the concourse, among the officials who swarmed around as I climbed out. I hardly recognized him at first. With an identity card pinned to a pale grey blazer, tie, and hair parted in the middle and wet with enough water to tone down the colour, he looked like just another official, though younger and greasier than most of them.

Before Mrs C came surging up with her screams and tears, he'd already taken my hand and solemnly kissed it. And with me in racing togs, chest heaving and hair plastered to my skull, this must have looked fairly odd. I fought back a ridiculous urge to play my part in this pageant and begin dancing a minuet with him, stately in dripping black racers, imagining the full, hooped skirt, the white wig. 'What are you *doing* down here?' I asked.

'Saluting you, before you get ambushed,' he said. 'Norm said it was on the cards. Woman, you *were third*. Believe it. You won the bronze. You'll be standing on the victory dais. I'll see you after your 400 metre event.'

I gulped. He expected me to remember my 400 metre event, *now*? He stood aside for Bulldog, who was weeping and ecstatic and obviously didn't recognize him. I was conscious of his eyes watching as I put on my track suit and had my hand shook over and over in Italian and every other language and began to believe it and waited for the pandemonium to subside.

Dawn Fraser had her own victory party going already among the green blazers and track suits. The American group around Chris Von Saltza was quieter. I'd gathered up Bulldog and Mr Upjohn, and unbeknown to them, a ghostly, smiling watcher. Eventually I was asked to come to the other end of the pool for the victory ceremony.

With the main lights turned off, we were just three in the spotlight, waiting for our names and to step onto the dais, with the Olympic flame burning in a bowl nearby and the pool, now calm, stretched out before us.

After trumpets, announcements in Italian, a little parade of V.I.P.s and girls in grey dresses carrying the medals on cushions, 'Dawnie' and her koala stepped up for gold and Chris for silver.

I heard my name called out. I stepped up onto the box marked 3, and bent down as a Very Important Man in a suit put the gleaming medal, hung on a chain of leaves, around my neck. As they played the Australian anthem, we turned to watch the three flags go up: the Australian Southern Cross with five stars, and lower, the New Zealand one with four, and the Stars and Stripes. All red, white, and blue, floodlit against the black sky.

Need I say, I was thinking of family, Mr Jack, Andy, Maggie, even Maggie's sad Mum, even Miss Macrae, even Keith, my whole parade of people, and a man with his Titian hair parted in the middle, watching. My eyes were dripping water and I couldn't stop smiling.

What then do I remember? The crowd breaking out again, Dawn Fraser leaning down to congratulate her arch-rival and then the kid from Down Under. About a million flash bulbs went off. The picture they used on the front page of the paper at home showed Dawn centre, arms around Chris on the right, me on the left — grinning like the Cheshire Cat, clutching my little Maori doll, a present from my sister Debbie — all of us wearing our medals around our necks. The pool lights came up. Time for the next race, to move on, exit centre back. We were wanted in the interview room. I might have caught a last glimpse of Tom by the tunnel entrance. Or was it some other official with a clipboard and a centre parting? Or, in all this drama, had I imagined the minuet?

States of exile

Like Eliza Doolittle at the ball, 'I knew that she could do it, and indeed she did!'

I watched, with increasing delight and tension, her first two races. She could match her rivals for sheer speed, and could outdo most of them when it came to sorting out the winners and losers in the final twenty yards. Simple observation and logic told me that the bronze medal was not out of her reach.

Beside me, Norm Thompson, laconically recording her progress towards the final, had reached the same conclusion: that behind Fraser and Von Saltza, 'the bronze is up for grabs'. But by Monday night, the watching from afar and sending of notes (and charms for her bracelet I cannot really afford) had become intolerable. In the excitement of the men's semi-final event prior to hers, it took only the quick swipe of an official blazer discarded on the back of a chair, borrowing the tie from around Norm's neck, a clipboard from a desk, a rearrangement of hair, to gain admittance to the concourse.

Down there, among a small army of grey-blazered officials, it was the difference between watching an opera from the dress circle and being on a vast stage in the second row of the chorus. She walked in seventh, virtually unknown except to those few of the vast crowd who declared themselves from the floodlit heights as New Zealanders. I knew I should not, must not let her see me, but she had gone into a private world, a trance which could have been concentration, or just sheer terror.

How I felt for her! States of exile: the indescribable loneliness of the singer waiting for an entry, an actor for a cue, the student to begin an exam, the athlete about to throw five years of back-breaking work into one race, one jump, the woman beginning labour. Adrenalin pumping, and no escape.

Alessandra, standing motionless behind the block, unlike your restless rivals, you were well named Archer. You were Diana as archer and bow, her glorious arrow.

It took every bit of self-control I possessed not to fling my arms around her when she finally climbed from the water. I could see she had suspended belief in the result. The grey eyes registered amusement when she recognized me. In the uproar of the finish, kissing her wet hand before Mrs Churchill came panting over, I was able to tell her that she'd better believe it, because it was obvious she didn't.

I long for her second race to be over, to find out what goes on behind those deep-set grey eyes; what sort of a fifteen-year-old comes to her first international meeting and, apparently unperturbed, walks off with a bronze medal; what she will make of problems which, like Eliza Doolittle's, are only just beginning; why she stirs in me thoughts of my homeland better left forgotten.

Aftershock

For days, everything blurred. It's my diary that tells me I went to
the interview room and talked to Norm Thompson and lots of
other reporters that night. Talked into a microphone for
someone from the New Zealand Broadcasting Service. Talked
and tried to describe my medal to the family and Mr Jack
laughing down the phone from home: there's this boy being
carried on people's shoulders through a crowd, it's lovely, the
colour is, well, *bronze.*

According to my diary I did go training the next day, and again
on Wednesday morning, trying to hide from gushing people like
the Australian chaperone with the voice like Donald Duck. I
really tried to raise some enthusiasm for the 400 metre heats.
It'd never been my distance. Maggie had won the last one I'd
raced, back in February. This time everything caught up with
me. My heat wasn't until nearly 10.30 at night. There were two
false starts, I got a mouthful on the dreaded fifth lap and my legs
just about dropped off. My time was 1.2 seconds off my best,
tenth fastest, respectable enough. I tried, but I'm a sprinter.
They give the men a 200 metre race, why not the women? I
didn't tell my diary I was not sorry to be watching the final from
the competitors' stand. I'd done my dash.

Imagine the bliss of waking very late, that morning of the final
I didn't have to swim, knowing I didn't have to go training
today, tomorrow, or even too seriously next week for the Naples
carnival on the 13th. No training, I wanted to shout out the
window. NO TRAINING. YaHOO.

Thursday, nearly noon. I lay dozing. I've done my job, Tom,
what magic thing is next, this first of September? How long can
you stay floating about on cloud nine? It had not all been a

fantastic dream; I had the medal and fifty thousand telegrams hanging over the dressing-table mirror to prove it. Tom had not been a figment of my imagination; I had yesterday's laurel wreath on my bracelet. He'd only sent a message via Norm Thompson after my 400m heat — 'A valiant swim. Sleep well. Lunch tomorrow.' Why not here, now, in person, damn you? I remembered the sleek Italian who'd been there at the finish. God knows how he'd talked his way onto the concourse looking like just another official. A chameleon — that's it, a lounge lizard. Perhaps the music student from New Zealand didn't exist either. Why should I believe that any more than the two Italian versions I'd seen already? Impostor, rich English boy good at accents, playing jokes, looking for an easy girl and a cheap thrill to remember the Olympics by? Perhaps the bracelet was cheap silver plate in a false box? The hair a wig?

Enter Tommaso. I'd just sat down to lunch and was downing a huge glass of Coke when he sauntered into the dining hall, looking more Italian than ever, carrying a vast bunch of gold, orange and bronze flowers. Carnations, roses, orchids, done up with gypsophila and greenery, bronze-coloured ribbons, everything but bells and whistles. This joker in his canary yellow shirt with paler hat to match didn't do things by halves.

'Lover boy himself,' murmured Zoe across the table. The men, except for Mr Upjohn who went on eating and looked askance at the flowers, hailed him like a long-lost friend. 'Tommaso, mio amico, where ya bin?' He bowed and scraped and shook some hands. 'Flowers for the little lady,' they teased, because there was no doubt who they were for. I might be youngest in the team, but mine was the only medal so far.

He waited till I stopped choking, then I was treated to another kiss on the hand, his eyes as bland as butter. He saw the race on television, he explained to everyone. He came directly from his office in Milano. 'Alessandra, bambina mia, you were magnificent. A star! Una campionessa. Magneefica!'

I was too furious even to say grazie. Bambina mia! The flowers were too big to put on the table or even across my lap, so I propped them against the window and listened to him say his lines. Alas, he must work for the Rome office of his company, but tomorrow, 'tomorrow I go to watch Signor Halberg and Signor Snell, another one 'oo is big surprise'. He apologized for Rome being so unusually hot for her visitors, and asked about the team's fortunes so far. Having given the child her flowers, he sipped discreetly at a cup of cappuccino, listening, ignoring me; paying, if anything, more attention to Zoe who wasn't acting at all like someone engaged.

'You can come with us,' Bulldog said suddenly. Her mind worked rather slowly in the heat. 'Alex and I are going to the athletics tomorrow. We've got a spare ticket.' He'd be delighted, signora. They arranged it all between them, Bulldog flirting, in on the joke. Mr Upjohn looked unimpressed. The bambina sat and fumed. I'd thought he might work up enough enthusiasm to come with us to the 400 metre finals tonight, but it wasn't mentioned. I didn't dare, myself, unless we could get alone somewhere, and that looked unlikely. I gathered up my bouquet and made a grand exit. I had, I said, some letters to write.

Perhaps, I thought angrily, he'd forgotten all about Roma out there to be explored.

Well, the 400 metres was Chris Von Saltza's triumph. Like Dawn Fraser, she'd had years of local, state, and national events, fighting off challengers all the way up. I'd had an easy ride, one rival only. I could never swim like that, or like the men in the other events. They all looked so tough and battle-scarred. For the first time I found myself wondering how much longer I wanted to go on.

At breakfast the next morning Murray Halberg, our best chance for a gold, and Peter Snell, who had unexpectedly made the 800 metre final, sat silent, apart from the team. They just nodded when people said 'good luck, guys'. I had a message to wait for Mr Upjohn. He wanted to see me, something very important.

The Bulldog, clucky over Tommaso's reappearance, and pleased that I'd given her some of the flowers for her room, went off to do her washing. We were to meet up with Tom at the main entrance later. I found a sunny corner of the hall and dozed deliciously. Five minutes before closing time Mr Upjohn came through the doors and piled up his tray as usual.

'Morning, Alex,' he said, looking pointedly at my bare legs. I pulled down skirt and crossed legs in a manner proper for Listening to Important Messages. 'I had to wait for a call through to New Zealand.'

Porridge, followed by sausages, eggs, and bacon, in this heat! I could hear his jaws going, between bursts of talk. This was going to be a long conversation. Two weeks of Italian food — he'd put on weight.

'How would you like to go to America, Alex?' he said, at last, as to a five-year-old.

'When?'

'I've been approached by a top administrator from a Californian university. There's talk of offering you a swimming scholarship. We're to meet him and a Mr Hoover, midday at the pool.'

'Sorry, I can't.' He spluttered on his sausage. 'Not at midday, I'm going to the athletics today.'

He put down his knife and fork and looked at me. 'Alex, this is a serious offer. I said you'd be available to discuss it.'

'I'm not, at least not . . .' American swimming scholarship? What every swimmer dreams of. Was I barmy?

'I can't go back and say you've just gone to watch the athletics.'

'It's not just the athletics, it's Murray Halberg and . . .' It was also seeing Tom again.

'I've just been on the phone to New Zealand. You're still very young of course. The proposal is for next September, when their college year starts. That won't interfere with the coming season in New Zealand. We're planning a team — this is highly confidential, Alex — to go to one of the Australian state meetings in January, and possibly their nationals in February. Of course, you'll be number one choice. I presume you're back at school next year, but leaving in September wouldn't . . .'

'What if I want to sit scholarship?' I said, simply to stop him.

'Scholarship? You mean at home? But we're talking of America. It's four years. You'd do a degree. You'd have to spend some holidays at home, to qualify for Perth in '62 and of course

110

Tokyo in '64, but I'm sure we can cope with that, when the time comes.' He smugly finished off the last of his croissants as I stared at him. 'These Yanks are very keen.'

And you've got it all worked out, I thought. 'Tell him I'll think about it.'

This time he really did splutter over his coffee.

'Alex, you don't just tell Americans you'll think about it!'

'They can't expect me to say yes *today*.'

'But they want to talk today.'

'I'm going to watch Murray Halberg.'

'They might see that as a casual and childish way to treat a good offer. They believe you have enormous potential for the gold in Tokyo.'

Back to his old pompous tricks. My head was in such turmoil — excitement, fright, *four* years more training, California here we come, what degree would I do, could it be law, Australia, Perth, Tokyo, four *years*, leave family, leave Mr Jack, leave school? — that I couldn't say anything. He thought I was just being difficult. He sighed, wiping the grease from his lips. 'Very well, Alex, I'll meet Mr O'Reilly and say . . . heaven knows what I'll say. Tell me a time when you will meet him.'

I couldn't have chosen a better day to have a vision of gold, and what it cost, waved in front of me.

I knew that both Murray Halberg and Peter Snell had trained for years with Arthur Lydiard round the Scenic Drive out at Titirangi, about twenty miles like a roller-coaster through native bush. I'd been out there a couple of times with Andy in the Vee-Dub. You get some great views of the city. They said only the toughest runners survived the circuit.

What would be my 'drive' for gold — eight, ten miles a day? Five hours in the water and no scenery? In a sunlit all-year pool in California or various dreary pools in Auckland? Or not at all?

'You're quiet today,' said Tom as the stadium, nearly full for a big day, shimmered around us and just below, the runners prepared for the 800 metre final, one of the glamour events. 'Snell must be the big muscly one in black?'

I nodded. It was true I hadn't said much as we walked over to the stadium. Bulldog grumbled about the heat as usual. Once

111

away from the village, Tommaso was Tom. We were politely distant. I should have been on top of the world.

Watching first Peter and then Murray run to golds had a most strange effect on me. Peter was only 21, with big ears and not forthcoming at the best of times, an outsider. No one in the seats round us thought he had a snowflake's chance. At one stage he was only fifth. Then he moved up to third. Sprinting for the finish the miracle happened — he found a gap between the two leading runners and hurtled between them towards the tape like a bullet. Once through, his balance and rhythm came completely unstuck. He changed from champion to gawky kid trying to stay upright, then wrapped himself around a flagpole, looking stunned. The runner who came second hunched himself up on the ground and cried.

At the end of the 5000 metres, Murray Halberg took two steps across the finish and collapsed. He'd gone from last, to second, then with three laps to go, into a huge lead. I heard people round us scream, 'He's gone too soon, he's mad. They'll get him in the last lap.' It was torture to watch, as Murray kept looking back at the second runner catching him, but he still had about ten yards to spare at the finish. The whole stadium was on its feet, bellowing. Peter Snell in his black track suit and a panama hat ran over and knelt down to congratulate our second Olympic champ of the day. It was the first big-time running I'd ever seen, so much more exposed and changeable than swimming. I could see how judging pace and tactics were as important as mere speed.

And in the end, wasn't there also a special 'something' that separates the champions from the rest? These two runners had it, Dawn Fraser had it, and Chris Von Saltza. Did I? Or was my bronze a flash in the pan? Could I go to America and spend four years working towards Tokyo and find I didn't have what it took?

I hadn't actually wept when I'd stood on my bronze dais. Nor since, not real teeming buckets. Now, the Olympic fanfares sounded that trumpet tune we were all getting to know rather well. Twice within an hour, two small black figures out there had stepped up onto the victory dais. The same people who sat staring at their breakfast this morning, now heroes. Our flag went up and our anthem rang out twice.

By then, I was a mess. A stadium full of people from all over the world stood to salute the winners, our winners. You could see small pockets of New Zealanders waving flags and going berserk. We'd never had an Olympic day like it. Two of the big events in quick succession. Possibly we never would again. People from big countries like America and Russia and Britain and France and Japan and Germany and Australia *expect* their athletes to win lots of medals — they could *never begin* to understand what it meant to people from a little place.

As the tumult died down, people in front of us were turning round to stare. Was I a sister, a girlfriend? Tom handed me a hanky and Bulldog tried to cuddle me. Behind my straw hat I cried for what those two athletes had just done, and what I had done, and what it had cost them pounding for years round the Scenic Drive and me up and down the Tepid Baths. I cried because I was surrounded by strangers and scared stiff of the whole new world of choices and responsibilities I'd opened up. America, university, school? Another season, Australia, or retire now? Trust Tom, or not? Trust myself? Wait for him to make the next move, or not?

'Better now, dear?' asked Bulldog, oozing sympathy. 'Do you want to go home?'

'Yes. No. Home, where's that? I don't know.'

'I think,' said Tom finally, as some huge Russian women heaved black steel balls into the air, and my embarrassing waterfalls dried to a trickle, 'I think what you need is a fair dinkum holiday.'

'Someone wants me to go to America,' I sniffed. Out of the corner of my eye, I saw him look away, as people do when they don't want you to see their face. 'Next year. A swimming scholarship.'

'Congratulations,' he said; without enthusiasm, I thought. 'That's terrific.' It was only later, as we ambled across the bridge back to the village, that he finally got around to suggesting that next year would take care of itself. Perhaps tomorrow I could think of myself as being on holiday, and what about starting with the Forum?

Full-length on the warm grass beneath a headless statue of a vestal virgin, I listened to the rich voice. No training. No Bulldog. Just me and Tom, the sights of Rome and/or the rest of the Olympics to pick and choose from. I wiggled my toes. I could smell roses, hear doves cooing and water trickling into the three marble pools in the courtyard where once the vestal virgins walked.

' "There were only six vestal virgins at one time," ' read Tom, fluently translating from an Italian guidebook. ' "Aged from 15 to 45, they were selected from aristocratic families, and lived in a spacious atrium house in the shadow of the Palatine hill." Up there. "Their primary function was to, ah, tend the sacred fire of Vesta in the nearby circular Temple." That's the white ruin with the four pillars, over there.'

'How did you manage to persuade Bulldog that she didn't have to tag along?'

'I'm very convincing. I come from an old Taihape farming family. She knows my aunt in Christchurch, a city councillor, JP, pillar of the Anglican church. She trusts me. "The Virgins were, um, bound by a strict rule of chastity. Punishment for failure of duty was harsh . . ." '

'She's a gullible old snob. You're also male and breathing.' He smiled as he went smoothly on.

' ". . . earning a beating by a priest if the sacred fire was allowed to go out, or death by burial alive if a Virgin broke her vow of chastity." '

'Yuk. Like Aida and whatsisname.'

'Radames. You know it?'

'We listened one night at home, Mum's crash course in Italian opera. The whole three hours. I had the words. Fantastic.'

'In that case, you will accompany me to see the open-air production at the Terme di Caracalla next Tuesday.'

I giggled. 'You do me much honour, sir.' The sky above was blinding blue, and the dry grass prickled my bare arms. I put my hat over my face. Opera in Rome!

' "The Virgins were not however secluded like nuns. They enjoyed the rare privilege of driving around Rome in carriages, and were honoured guests at all public functions and spectacles. They were" ah . . . "confidantes of the Emperors, and used their considerable power to influence public affairs." '

114

'Sounds a pretty good sort of life,' I mumbled sleepily. 'Perhaps I was a vestal virgin in a previous life. Mixing with the nobs on the Palatine, best seats at the Circus Maximus, driving around in a carriage.'

'What about the chastity bit?'

'What about it? I'm not going to marry either. Or have sprogs,' I said propping myself up on my elbows. 'I like this place. It feels, well, female.' There were dragonflies hovering about the pools, red roses and bougainvillaea climbing over ruined brick walls. Behind the row of female statues (even if only one of them had a head) were lots of trees and pink oleanders. This corner of the Forum was quite different from the rest we'd already explored with the aid of Tom's guidebook. I'd walked on the stones of the Via Sacra, and touched a sandalled foot, just a foot, growing weirdly out of a block of marble, and taken pictures of the pillars against the sky. I had to keep reminding myself where I actually was.

'How did the American interview go?' Tom asked softly.

'Oh okay.' I flopped onto my side, away from him. I met Mr Upjohn and two Americans first thing after breakfast, which was taken over by a crowd of reporters and photographers after Snell and Halberg. 'It was quite strange, really. This old American guy from San Francisco, he spoke so softly I could hardly hear him. He asked me all sorts of questions about my family, and my interests, and how Mr Jack would feel if I went. Training schedules, the pools I trained in. What I want to be . . .'

'Which is?'

'Lawyer. I've always wanted to do law. Anyway, Mr Upjohn kept interrupting and asking about contracts and expenses and money, and this guy just quietly kept asking me questions about school and stuff. He was so polite and old-fashioned he should have been English. Kept calling me Miss Archer and offering me coffee.'

'They're not all loud of mouth and tie, you know.'

'I really liked him. He said because I was so . . .' Did Tom still think I was eighteen? '. . . relatively young, I'd stay with a selected family for the first year, then I'd stay on campus. They'd pay for all my tuition, books, everything except travel to and from the States.'

After a long pause he said 'Sounds great. How can you refuse.'

'Are you here on a scholarship?'

'Not exactly.'

'What does that mean?'

'After I finished my degree, I worked for seven months. Seagull on the wharves, waiter, night-watchman. Hospital orderly for a few weeks. Piano and theory teacher, which I detested. The brats never practised. I saved quite a bit, I had to. It was quite something to be accepted as a pupil in Milan, but no money went with it.'

Something didn't add up: the poor student one minute and now the smooth Italian clothes, the bracelet around my wrist, the air of money.

'Did you accept?' he asked. 'The scholarship?'

'I wasn't asked to, really. They're going to send the details. After this summer, Australia, all that . . .' I felt more tired than excited by a prospect that was too big to even contemplate. 'No one's interested in me anymore,' I said sleepily. 'They all want to talk to Snell and Halberg now, thank goodness. I'm a has-been.'

I was on holiday, and at eleven-thirty in the morning in the Forum Romanum underneath a headless vestal virgin I must've drifted off to blissful sleep. '*Sic transit gloria mundi,*' I heard him say quietly. 'Wait till you get home.'

Notes of caution

It has taken Alex these past four days to wind down, and even then I don't think I am seeing more than a glimpse of the real personality. She is too far away from home, too precariously suspended between the climax of her unexpected success yet having to continue training, between the restrictions of middle-aged guardians and wanting to be on holiday in Rome. As far as I can tell, no real friends.

Except, if she will allow it, me.

The 400 metre heats were, frankly, a tiresome procession; eight lengths and the winners clearly obvious by the end of the first two. In the third and last heat, very late at night, she looked tired, as did Dawn Fraser herself, swimming with none of the fire of her sprint events. Norm, beside me, watching her struggle over the eight lengths of very rough water, said she'd never liked the longer distances. Cyril Upjohn had told him she was finding the inevitable feeling of anticlimax difficult. She had not taken kindly to his insistence that she must keep training for the invitation meeting in Naples the week after next.

She certainly received my salutation of flowers coolly enough. I could think of no alternative to resuming my Tommaso role if I wanted to get into the New Zealand dining hall. Telephones and messages in the village office are a less than reliable way of making contact. At lunch she was offhand, giving me no chance to make any arrangements before making an admittedly grand exit; and again at the stadium until the victory ceremony for Snell and Halberg. I have no idea what accumulated tensions were finally being released; from Mrs Churchill's guarded comments and her solicitude, from Norm Thompson's hints of a bumpy ride in the run-up to Rome, I guess they were considerable. One forgets so easily that she is not yet sixteen. She is not someone who makes life easy for herself, and never will be. I still long to find out what makes her tick — these precious days in Rome will be too short.

And how does one reconcile her returning to school, the prospect of America next September, with my staying in Milan next year and Europe possibly for ever? Her obvious and untested love for our homeland and my abhorrence of it? Her tender age and my worldly 23? Her declared ambition to do law, meaning five straight years at varsity, and my musicial ambitions, a capricious career at best.

Since I can see no way through this tangle, some caution, some other masks are called for.

A walking encyclopaedia

Everything about the man who had just parked his motor scooter under the flagpoles and was now walking my way yelled Australian.

The wide-brimmed bush hat, the garish green shirt with the Sydney harbour bridge plastered all over it, the jeans, the boots, the swagger with arms swinging like an ape. As he got closer he tipped his hat slightly back, revealing a thick gingerish moustache and sunglasses. There were plenty of Aussie males loose in Rome for the Games. About three yards away he stopped. I could feel his eyes behind the sunglasses swivelling up and down, then he gave a soft whistle. I was just about to tell him to clear off when he said, 'G'day, Kiwi.'

'Oh God,' I said. 'Not again. Will you stop doing that!'

'Any self-respecting Aussie . . .' said Tom.

'You're not an Aussie and you're late.'

'Yes, apologies. No excuses. I had to iron my shirt.'

'Where *did* you get that gear? It's awful.'

'Glad you approve. I came here by ship. The *Fairstar*, Italian. We stopped at Sydney, Perth, Colombo, Bombay, Aden, Suez, and Port Said.'

'I suppose you bought Indian . . . what do you call them?'

'Dhotis? Shalwar kameez?'

'And Egyptian robes and those silly red hats like flower pots . . .'

'Fez. Oh yes, I could have gone to the ship's fancy dress as a white slave trader . . . As a matter of fact, I went in drag. The thought of joining the usual corps de ballet doing *Swan Lake* in crepe paper didn't appeal. I upstaged all of them by going as a tiddly over-the-hill opera singer, singing *Carmen* in falsetto.

You can do that sort of thing when you're alone. That gear I *did* have to borrow — the wig, the frilly frock.'

'I should hope so.' I saw two of our team men come out of the village entrance, notice me and wave. 'Look, if you expect me to get on the back of that scooter incognito, you'd better go somewhere less public.'

'I'll wait round the corner,' he said, moving swiftly to fire up the machine and roar off as the two athletes came over. They wondered if I needed rescuing! Perhaps I did, I thought, though not quite as they imagined.

It was ten minutes before their bus came and I could walk round to where Tom was waiting under a tree, still sitting on the Vespa and reading an Italian newspaper. 'Aussies can't read Italian papers,' I said.

'Aussie Italians can. Or should that be Italian Aussies?'

I looked at the scooter doubtfully. It didn't look too new or strong. 'Where did you get this thing?'

'A friend. It won't do more than 20 miles per hour, but it'll get us around for the next week. Hop on.'

'Bulldog wouldn't like it.'

'Bulldog's not going to get it. Hop on.' I climbed on the back. 'Have you never ridden pillion before? Grip with your knees as in horse-riding and grab me round the waist. This city has lots of cobblestones and bumps. Tighter.'

Apart from frequent hand-kissing, it was the first actual bodily contact. If I'd expected from his stocky shape that he'd be slightly soft and cuddly around the middle, I was totally wrong. The stomach muscles under the thin shirt were rock-hard, as hard as any athlete's. All those singer's breathing exercises, I supposed.

Over his shoulder, I saw his hand go out to turn the key, and hesitate. He half turned in the seat. Our faces were very close, his hand was under my chin and he was after a kiss.

'May I?' he said very softly, his eyes already half closed in anticipation.

'It's only nine in the morning,' I said, recoiling.

'Does that matter?'

'That silly moustache does.'

120

He ripped it off, and rubbed at where it had been with the back of his hand. 'Now, is that better?'

'No.' Why? I thought. Why not?

He turned back, paused for a long moment, stuck the moustache back on, started the scooter, and we moved off. He was right, it wasn't Speedy Gonzales. I gripped him round his rock-hard waist and thought oh hell, what happens now? Am I hanging onto one of those guys who think that money spent on taking girls for meals and movies equals kisses, and more? Is that the week shot to pieces already?

'So where are we going?' he shouted.

'I'm paying my own way this week,' I shouted in his ear. I could feel my breasts hard against his back, and no doubt he could too.

'You don't have to yell. That's what I expected.' Then I saw his wrists working the handlebar controls and we puttered to a stop under another tree. We hadn't even gone two hundred yards. He didn't turn around.

'We'd better set some ground rules, Alessandra. Okay, we're going Dutch, money-wise, museum tickets, Cokes, everything. That's fine by me. You can make the next move, kissing-wise, if you want to. I don't see why it should always be the male. Frankly, it's caused me no little embarrassment and distress over the years. I'm sorry, I moved too quickly. I won't again.'

'That's okay,' I mumbled, still acutely conscious of my front pressing hard against the picture of the Sydney harbour bridge, the warmth of his back, the fresh smell of shampoo. Perhaps we'd have been safer getting around Rome on a bus, in more ways than one.

'Can you teach me to drive this thing?' I asked.

'Why not?'

Bulldog would have a double fit!

That Sunday was two weeks after our first lunch date, six days after my bronze medal and two days after I became convinced that Tom was, for whatever reason and whoever he really was, serious as in *serious* about me.

We went back to St Peter's and explored it properly, along with about four million other people. I was glad he'd told me last night to bring a cardigan, because women with sleeveless dresses were not allowed in. Some, looking sheepish, wore their husband's jackets to get past grim-looking men in robes posted like police under the huge bronze doors. We stood and listened to a service going on in Latin, with the organ and male choirs singing loudly and flat. People around us crossed themselves frequently and whispered in Latin and went up to get the Communion. Tom stood very still, his face politely blank; so he wasn't a Catholic. I noticed lots of pale teenage boys in robes with their heads shaved, and thin girls in veils and dowdy dresses; trainee priests and nuns, I supposed. We walked on marble of every possible colour, grey, green, pink, brown, black, orange, and marvelled at the mosaics, and stood speechless and misty-eyed in front of the Pietà, so much smaller than I'd imagined, and climbed up 330 steps to the very top of the dome.

The city lay around us in a haze of heat, the buildings all earthy-pink and the Vatican gardens and the hills all tree-green. I thought of my nights on the village rooftop, looking at this very dome like a pearl against the black sky.

'How do you cope with it, all this glorification! Are you a believer?' he said suddenly as we leant, still sweating, over the railing on the side shaded from the sun.

'In what?'

'God. The Trinity, the Virgin birth, Christmas, Easter, all that. *In hoc spero.*'

'Are you?'

'You haven't answered my question, but no, I'm not, despite years of church schools. I sang in choirs, from boy soprano down to bass, every part and all the solos. High Anglican church music is unsurpassed. But I grew tired of ritual, signifying nothing. Those medieval mysterious services going on below us seem worse.'

'Life after death?'

'It seems like wishful thinking to me. People live on in their children, their memories, their life work. A genius like Michelangelo leaves behind a little more.' He waved at the great open arms of the square below, where the people looked like ants and buses like toys. 'I shall leave satisfied audiences and recordings of my voice.'

'I've got a bronze medal,' I said lightly. 'So far.' We laughed. This surprising conversation was getting too close to questioning my conviction that Andy's spirit still lived somewhere. 'I think . . . making the most of what you've got, or been given . . .'

'Then you're a humanist.'

'I wouldn't know. I don't want to be anything "ist".'

'A free spirit.'

'I suppose so. I hope so.'

'They'll clip your wings, when you get home.'

'That's the second time you've said that. Why?'

'Our homeland is suspicious of success. Especially those who make it big overseas.'

'That's nonsense. Think of Ed Hillary. The papers will be full of Snell and Halberg.'

'For a few days. You will have your moment of glory. I'm not actually talking about the newspapers. Despite all their noble intentions they deal in half-truths, half-lies, and all the shifting sands in between. As you probably well know.'

'What then?' This was serious stuff for the top of St Peter's dome.

'Sufficient unto the day.' From his back pocket he brought out a small book. 'Lord Byron again. *Childe Harold's Pilgrimage*, a journey through Europe, published in its entirety, 1818. I read it last night. Listen to what he says about St Peter's dome, upon which we stand . . .

Thou movest, but increasing with the advance,
Like climbing some great Alp, which still doth rise,
Deceived by its gigantic elegance;
Vastness which grows, but grows to harmonise —
All musical in its immensities;
Rich marbles, richer painting — shrines, where flame
The lamps of gold — and haughty dome which vies
In air with Earth's chief structures, though their frame
Sits on the firm-set ground, and this the clouds must claim.

123

What do you think of that?'

'Not bad.' Actually, I couldn't quite understand it. 'Read it again.' He did, while I looked down at the curve of "the haughty dome". If it was plain old *awe* Lord Byron was trying to get across, he succeeded. Tom finally broke the spell.

' "Some great Alp" — well, this climber needs a beer, and badly.' We walked once more round the circular balcony, and then set off again down the curving stone staircase. *Silence=death* was scratched on a wall. And lower down, *JFK for President, I hate Dean Martin,* and *Giorgio è stupido.*

As we walked across the main steps, I noticed Tom was chewing gum and had slipped into his Aussie cowboy walk, which may have been because, in all those thousands of people, we banged into five of my New Zealand team-mates. Next thing, he was shaking hands and introducing himself as my Aussie cousin Dennis ('on her mother's side, she's my father's sister, her mother that is, gettit mate!') in a convincing Oz accent. He was living at Earl's Court in London, working as a barman, but had to come and see his little cousin swim in the Games. 'Went like a bomb, didn't you, cuz,' slapping me on the shoulder.

'And how did youse guys get on?' They were hockey players — weren't doing too bad, considering, might end up fifth. 'I bet youse guys are proud of my little Kiwi cuz. Ran rings around them, didn't you girlie? Except for our Dawnie of course, and that American sheila. Got what it takes, I reckon, eh guys?' Sure, sure, they said, hot and tired and embarrassed by his enthusiasm, even from an Aussie. And from behind his sunglasses I caught the look which said *See what I mean?*

Tom made this deal with Bulldog. That we had to be back in the village each night before dark, unless we'd made special cast-iron arrangements involving taxis and times. She'd teamed up with Mr Upjohn and one of the Australian women to go sightseeing, so she was happy.

I made a deal with Mr Upjohn. Now I was worth asking, we'd been summoned to Naples for a special invitation meeting on Tuesday week. It meant I had to keep training, but we agreed I could go every morning at 6.30. Actually, walking over the bridge was no pain, with the river golden and misty in the new sun, and by the time I got there it was so hot and close that the mile in the water was pure pleasure. Only a few swimmers turned up each morning. I kept telling myself: I am the third fastest woman in the world!

I was stuck with the Australian Tom, though I was relieved that for the rest of the week he toned it down to ordinary shirts without the Sydney harbour bridge, and only a slight hint of the cowboy walk. I thought he was overdoing the bit about Tommaso not getting found out. It was only a joke, but he was dead serious. 'What I start, I see through,' he said. Or perhaps he just enjoyed dressing up. I got quite used to the moustache. It was amazing how completely different he looked.

After our St Peter's day we had Monday to Saturday to explore Rome. We did all the touristy things, rode down the Via Condotti and sat on the Spanish Steps and threw our coins in the Trevi Fountain, visited the Vatican and the Sistine Chapel, the Pantheon and the Campidoglio and museums until even I felt I'd had enough of marble statues and friezes and sarcophagi.

Well, I saw them, and smelt them, and took photos on my Zeiss Ikon to prove it. But my diary doesn't record the extras — the piazzas and side roads we explored, the little cafés and trattorias we discovered.

Tom said it was his first time in Rome, and I suppose this was true, but armed with his books and knowledge of things Italian, and getting into easy conversation with waiters and shopkeepers, it was like having a private guide. I obviously had a partner, so no one tried to pinch my backside. I was used to people staring more or less rudely because of my height, but here they stared and smiled and said 'Buon giorno, signorina', or 'Bellissima', and seemed to approve.

Tom talked a good deal of the time: facts, history, anecdotes connected with this or that building, statue, painting, fountain, piazza, villa. What he didn't know, he insisted on translating from his guidebooks. Pushing the bike down narrow lanes, well off the tourist track, he pointed out shady courtyards of private houses; decorated bronze doors and wrought-iron lamps; female figures with bare breasts, or male ones with muscles, carved into buildings, holding up archways or roofs; a bougainvillaea blazing against a brick wall; a tiny altar with lighted candles and a picture of the Virgin Mary built into a gateway. We wandered around markets full of strange vegetables, fantastical scarlet and gold peppers, red lettuces, baskets of nuts, figs, melons, chestnuts, and dried fruits. Even ordinary old lemons and peaches and cherries seemed bigger and brighter under orange canopies than they ever did in our boring shops at home.

We wandered in and out of cheese shops, delicatessens, and cake shops, fish shops and butchers' shops and wine shops and leather shops and shoe shops. I came out reeling with the ripe, sweet, dusty smells, utterly amazed at how many varieties of cheeses and salamis and fish and pastries, wine and shoes and leather bags they could pile into shops that looked so insignificant from the outside.

Tom would get into conversation with the shopkeepers, telling them about emigrating to Australia after the war, when he was just a boy of ten. I was introduced as an athlete from Nuova Zelanda who'd just won a medal at La Grande Olimpiade. That would set off much handshaking and noisy comments about (I think) my height and my youth and (possibly) my looks, while Tom jabbered away, and translated enough to keep me vaguely in the picture. Then we got to talking about the shopkeeper's family and we tasted this and tried that. I bought some goodies to take home as presents, and quite often I was given little goodies myself — jars of chestnuts in syrup, and gold-wrapped chocolates filled with liqueur. Family members were brought out from the back to meet us, and several times they asked Tom if he knew of long-lost relatives who had emigrated to Sydney in 1948. Sometimes it was half an hour or more before we left, glowing with heat and goodwill.

At frequent intervals we found small cafés for Cokes and big, crusty rolls filled with smoked ham and sweet tomatoes, followed by a gelato. How did one choose from fifty different flavours? Pale green pistachio? Pale yellow citron? Brown rum or mocha? *Liquorice?* We sat outside where we could. Tom consulted his books about the peculiarities of each district, while I listened to his rich, clear voice, and around us arguments, laughter, babies crying, horns and radios blaring; city life being lived, noisily and very publicly compared to

126

home. I saw street artists and street cleaners, and rows of ripped posters from the recent election, and fat Italian mommas and creased old men in berets, overdressed plump middle-aged women. Girls my age who looked like tarts, and slim teenage boys who, Tom told me, were the male version, and real ragged beggars. Many cats, and even more pigeons. I wondered where all the children were.

Once, after walking through the Borghese gardens, we went mad and paid a small fortune for a cup of coffee, just so we could sit at the yellow table of one of the smart outdoor cafés at the top of the Via Veneto. Tom had told me about the café society shown in a marvellous new film, *La Dolce Vita* — and here it was: bored old men in pale suits with young women in linen dresses, gloves, and hats like pillboxes or lampshades. Lonely Jewish ladies with wrinkled arms and lots of bracelets. Elegant young men in summer suits smoking thin cigars. Others, like us, pretending not to be tourists.

We sat for over two hours, analysing why some people looked elegant and others a mess, trying to guess their jobs, their families, their interests. Tom had a sharp eye for dress, I discovered. My own home-made blouses and skirts suddenly felt very simple and young and boring. I wondered what it really felt like to be 23 and made up like a film star and preening yourself in couturier clothes in the Via Veneto. They didn't look much happier for it.

Most days we had a late lunch in a trattoria, each time trying new antipasto, pasta, carne, pesce, vino, formaggio, caffè freddo or cappuccino, until we staggered sleepily back onto the trusty iron horse for the next short journey.

As well as his guidebooks, Tom bought Italian newspapers and translated extracts over lunch, so that I had a vague idea of what was happening in the Congo and the rest of the Games. Armin Hary, the German, and Wilma Rudolph, the tall American Negro girl I'd seen once or twice in the village, were winning the sprint events, and the Russians the gymnastics. A Greek prince had won a gold medal for yachting.

Oh yes, the Olympics! We thought of dropping in on the athletics or the weightlifting or the water polo down at the EUR complex, but in the end we just floated around Rome on our little motor scooter in a dream, not caring about the crowds or the sweltering heat or anything except the next drink or gelato, the next place to sit under a tree or umbrella, the next perfect little piazza or fruit market or gardens or unexpected small cool church.

He didn't once offer to help me off the bike, or hold my arm as we crossed roads, or attempt to hold my hand or put his arm around my shoulder Roman-style. He was a walking encyclopaedia on Rome, a closed book about anything to do with New Zealand, but easy to be with when neither of us felt like talking. Most nights we got back to the village as the light was fading, sticky and exhausted. At the gate, he kissed my hand, very formally, under the smirking gaze of the security guards; that was all.

One night I remember specially. You can blame the weather for lots of things.

On the Tuesday, we'd planned to walk down the Appian Way, visit the Catacombs and then come back to the Terme di Caracalla for the opera in the evening, all in the southern part of the city. I packed my best jacket-dress and some decent shoes to wear to the opera. Even at ten in the morning, even under the high stone walls and overhanging trees on either side of the Appian Way, the heat was incredible. After nearly two miles pushing the scooter over the stones worn smooth by Roman soldiers, we arrived at the catacomb place to find hundreds of people coming out. Presumably because the monks who ran it had to have a siesta, it was closed until four.

'I wouldn't mind a drink and just sleeping,' I said, and we did just that because it was too unbearably hot to do anything else. We flopped under a cypress tree in a wheat field next to the catacomb gardens. Real picture postcard stuff, families spreading picnic tablecloths among the wheat-stalks in the sun, except for fat grey cumulus clouds building up along the horizon. I dozed off listening to the children and dreaming of the impossible comfort of having my head on Tom's lap.

When I woke up the sky was grey all over, brewing up for something. Tom was sitting, staring into space, looking rather glum. I didn't dare mention the opera. Walking down the

128

Appian Way, he told me the whole plot of *Aida*, about the première in Cairo in 1871 for the opening of the new opera house and the Suez canal. Famous productions had three hundred extras, and elephants and camels walking across the stage for the Triumph scene.

I hated the Catacombs, which turned out to be underground cemeteries, not the hiding places I'd always thought they were. They smelled of death, and that's without any dead bodies! We went down with a whole bunch of English-looking people behind an English-speaking monk. Tom was unusually silent and I panicked about getting lost. I suppose the actual excavation was amazing, miles of deep, narrow corridors and alcoves for bodies, lit with gloomy red lights, but I couldn't wait to get out.

When we finally came up the last long flight of steps, it was nearly as black as it was below. We walked in silence to get the scooter. Tom tripped over a large stone in the road, bent down and threw it with surprising force into a hedge.

'Maybe it'll clear,' I said.

'Not a chance. Hundreds of chorus, dancers, musicians, the instruments . . . not a hope in hell.'

'Why don't we just go back to the Baths. Wait and see. Find a café or something? It might . . .'

'Sorry, Alex, but it won't. We'd better head back, take you home.'

'Isn't it worth . . .'

'No.' He was astride the scooter and firing it up. 'Hop on.'

'No,' I said. Tom was beginning to sound very like the uncouth Keith, ordering me around rudely. 'I still think . . .'

'Al*right*. We'll go to the Baths and see what happens.'

'Right.' But he knew Italian weather better than I did, and by the time we arrived at the Baths the sky was black, and thunder was rolling away. We rode around the outside of the ruins, already deserted. A large sign on a wire gate announced that the performance that night was *Annullata*, cancelled. The first fat drops of rain fell, with two fierce flashes of lightning, right over the city.

'We'd better go to my place,' he shouted over his shoulder as he set the scooter up a fairly steep hill. Halfway up, the sky fell in. The water was actually bouncing off the road. 'This is going to last for a while. We won't get back to the village.'

'How far, your place?' The thunder was directly overhead and continuous. There was one fearful flash of lightning, forking down between the trees. I was grabbing his waist *very* tightly. 'How *far*?'

'About a mile. I think I can find the way, coming from this direction.'

You'd better, I thought grimly, because Auckland doesn't have thunderstorms like this and I'm terrified. We were in streets of apartment buildings of four or five stories, with balconies and geraniums and climbing roses, wrought-iron gates, cars outside; no shops, cafés, any shelter except under dripping trees. The next flash of lightning, followed by a great thunderous crash like fifty million kettle drums, really worried me. I hung on tighter still and tucked my head in behind his broad back. Three more flashes and crashes, and I heard the motor slow down. We swung sharply over a kerb, to a stop.

'Hop off. Inside,' he said. 'Through that gate, turn right.' I dashed up a narrow alley towards a set of steps. He threw the scooter against a wall and ran up behind me. We looked at each other, drowned rats, shirts sticking, hats hanging down our backs, and laughed. Amazingly, the moustache was still firmly in place. He ripped it off, grimacing, and from his tight jeans produced two very large keys.

The entrance hall was gloomy, the lift antiquated, and the door to the apartment like a fortress. 'Go in,' he said, pushing the door open. 'Don't worry about the drips. It's all wood. Parquet.'

I went straight into the most beautiful room I'd ever seen, dark and formal. Tom took off his shoes, then padded round turning on some green and yellow lamps. The floors were honey-coloured wood, the walls and high ceilings pale gold. Each bit of furniture stood in its own space — chairs, a sofa, tables, a baby grand piano, a golden harp, wooden cabinets for music, hi-fi equipment, records, books. There were several Persian rugs, landscapes in gilt frames. The windows had long, draped, gold curtains and wooden shutters.

'You told me . . . I thought you meant a grotty student flat.'

'This belongs to a musician. A flautist, aunt of a friend in Milan. She played in one of the Rome orchestras.'

'Lucky you.'

'Sure. You'd better get those clothes off. I'll get you a dressing-gown.' He went off into another room, came out shirtless, carrying a cream cotton kimono and a towel. 'I'll ring the village, get a message through if I can. The bathroom's through there.' He was as full-chested as a surf swimmer, and somewhat browner than I'd imagined, him not being an outdoor person.

The bathroom was similarly huge, tiled, with built-in mirrors and cabinets. Basic toilet things inside the cabinets gave away nothing about the owner, or about Tom. I used one of the tortoiseshell combs, and wondered how I could look elegant in the kimono and not like an overgrown kid in a dressing-gown. Did I catch a look which said I'd succeeded without even trying, as I walked back into the living room?

'Does she live here alone?' I said.

'A son comes and goes. I gather the husband died in the war. There was money somewhere in the family.' Tom had put on clean beige trousers, a cream shirt. The hair I hardly ever saw was still wet and dark. We both looked rather sleek. He held out a tall glass of pale yellow wine. 'Wrap yourself around that.'

I tried not to giggle. Drinking wine in a kimono with nothing on underneath, alone with a sexy young man in a Roman flat? Bulldog would be having fifty thousand fits.

'I can't get through to the village,' he said. 'Power failure somewhere. Hardly surprising.' Even inside this solid room, the thunder was fantastically loud and the room was lit up every minute or so by the lightning. I walked over and peered out the window. The street below was flooded and the trees thrashed about in the wind.

'Sit down while I get some pasta cooked. The news comes on about now.' A cabinet turned out to be a small television, and after the newsreader, the first picture was the Olympic stadium, deserted. Tom listened to the announcer, then they showed maps of Italy and he snapped it off. 'They've had to stop the decathlon. They say they'll resume when the storm abates.'

The Olympic Games seemed a million miles away from this

room. I plucked a few strings of the harp, and looked at the baby grand. The music on it was a score, *Le Nozze di Figaro*, with lots of pencil marks on the singer's part — breath marks, > marks and < marks, *dim*s and *rit*s and various other reminders. Tom came back with a pottery bowl. 'Have a nut. Play if you want.'

'I'm rusty. How did you know I played?'

'Mrs Churchill mentioned talents besides your swimming, ballet, piano . . .'

'Only Grade 6! She's exaggerating.'

'Is she? Cin-cin!'

The wine was yellow and sweet. I wondered what else she'd let slip of my chequered past. What about his own?

'Will you sing something for me?' I asked. He walked away to the window. I thought, if you really are a singer, perhaps that's not the done thing, perhaps real students don't just sing for newish friends, like that. But he closed the shutters, turned on another two lamps, and went to the piano. After looking at the keys for a while, he picked up a music case sitting beside the stool and took out several books. Probably his own special music, brought from Milan.

I knew immediately, from the arpeggio accompaniment and the first few bars of the song, that he really could play and he really had a voice, a beautiful one. Whatever else, the singing student was for real. Sitting through all those recordings at home, I'd heard a fair few opera singers in the past year, and Tom's voice sounded as good as any of them. It was warm and seemed to be effortless, and made me think of rich, dark chocolate. He sang seven serious songs, one in French, two in German then four in Italian that sounded more operatic, although scaled down, taking the high notes in a sort of half voice.

Then he looked over at me, grinned and launched straight into 'I got Plenty of Nuttin', and 'Begin the Beguine' with a rumba-ish sort of accompaniment and his left foot tapping on the floor, and finally that Winnie-the-Pooh song 'How sweet to be a cloud, floating in the blue' . . . and by this time I knew he loved to sing as much, or more than, I loved to swim.

It was part of him, as much as the red hair or the smooth brown hands on the keys. I lay back on the settee in my cream kimono, sipping wine. Julia-at-school would be laughing herself silly, it's like something out of a *Woman's Weekly* serial, she'd be saying. But she'd be impressed too, the mellow Italian room, the bronze-haired man at the piano and his music, the storm outside. And envious. And scared stiff. What if I was twenty, not fifteen! What if . . .

This melting ache in my stomach. It was not what I expected to find in Rome. Or wanted ever again caused by someone who was too old for me, too smooth, too clever, too likely to fire me up and leave me swinging. From next week simply too far away. Not again.

'Who wrote the first ones?' I said.

'In order, Fauré, Schubert, Schumann. Mozart, Puccini, Verdi.'

'Do you know anything from *Aida?*' I asked.

'Ah. *Aida.*' He looked down at the keys. I knew the aria, 'Celeste Aida'. He sang it from memory, the accompaniment too, but quite softly. It sounds like a cliché, but I went goose-flesh at the high notes, especially the final one, dying away around the large room.

'I thought that was for a tenor,' I said, eventually. 'You said you were a baritone.'

'I sing the odd tenor piece, for fun.' Did I imagine that he went red under the freckles? 'When do you go? I'll see if I can get two more tickets.'

'Naples, on Monday, for three days. Back to New Zealand on Thursday. It'll have to be this week.'

'Damn the weather,' he said softly. If he was trying to get rid of some frustration, he chose a good piece to do it, loud and showy, Beethoven I think. He leapt off the stool. 'Recital's over. You play while I cook some pasta.'

The storm raged on for ages. I didn't play, not after what I'd just heard. We ate some spaghetti, with bolognese sauce out of a tin, drank more wine. A funny motheaten little dog with a pushed-up nose waddled in from the kitchen. 'Meet Turandot from Peking,' said Tom, 'the resident guard dog.' She seemed to like me. With Turandot on my lap, Tom on the floor, we listened to records of Maria Callas and especially of Tito Gobbi, Tom's total hero.

He also he showed me the music of the pieces he had sung, Schubert's 'Wohin?' and Schumann's 'Dichterliebe'. 'Non più andrai' from *The Marriage of Figaro*, Figaro sending Cherubino off to be a soldier. Don Giovanni's famous serenade, 'Deh, vieni alla finestra'. From *La Bohème*, 'Vecchia zimarra senti', frozen Colline parting company with his old coat to buy food for the dying Mimi. From *La Traviata*, Germont reminding his son about the beauties of their home in Provence, 'Di Provenza il mar, il suol'. None of them looked nearly as easy as he had made them sound. When I read the English words, and remembered the voice, I knew why they had all made me feel so sad.

Was it deliberate, that to show me the music he didn't sit beside me on the sofa, but knelt on the other side of the low table? That our hands met once on the music, his warm over mine, but I pretended not to notice? We both looked hard at the music and Tom went on with the involved plot of *Don Giovanni* and the moment passed.

He tried to contact the village again, and eventually got through to a distraught Mrs Churchill. She'd got caught in the storm in the Via Veneto, been robbed by a taxi-driver, and soon after she arrived a bolt of lightning had struck the village, ripping bits of concrete off the women's quarters, frightening the living daylights out of everyone.

He didn't quite tell her where we were. We both knew she would have flipped her lid, because people of her age always imagine the worst, young gels alone with a man, rape and such. 'We're having tea at a friend's place down near the Baths of Caracalla, in the area of the Monte Aventino,' he said, just slightly implying other company. I smiled, and kissed Turandot on her squashed nose. He'd call, he reassured her, for a taxi, but it might take an hour at least. Everyone would be wanting taxis after the storm. She was not to worry. This man was not dumb.

'We can go on the scooter,' he said, putting the telephone down. I started to say it was going to be a long ride for him, there and back, but he interrupted. 'Rome at night? After a monumental storm, the sort of storm that used to terrify the ancient Romans. It might be your only chance. Do you need any dry clothes?'

The Colosseum floodlit was literally out of this world. The

reflections and steam rising off the wet empty streets made it look like something out of an ancient dream, floating and ghostly. I was slightly steaming myself, in the damp and creased opera dress pulled from my bag and a jumper borrowed from Tom. I noticed he'd put on a jacket and scarf, as well as a sporting sort of cap. It had stopped raining, but the air was wet and cool, not good for singers, I imagine.

Without asking, Tom rode us around the Colosseum twice, and then very slowly along the road above the Forum, where the pillars shone silver and the archways of the Palatine ruins were all outlined with light, and past the white 'wedding cake'. Cars splashed through puddles and under trees weighted down with water, and the streetlamps cast pink and brown shadows.

The Via del Corso took us almost straight north to the Olympic village, or would have done. We did slight detours into fairyland, over the Tiber towards the Castel Sant' Angelo reflected in the river; twice around Saint Peter's Square, around the fountains, in and out of pillars and puddles; and back along the river up the Via Condotti to the Spanish Steps and back to the Piazza del Popolo, around the archway and the obelisk in the middle. We could have gone straight up the Via Flaminia, but somehow we found ourselves taking the long way up the right bank of the Tiber, crossing over the Ponte Duca d'Aosta, my bridge, to look down into the dark Stadio del Nuoto, my pool. Finally we walked over the Ponte Milvio, where I'd marched with the Olympic parade, and puttered the rest of the way to the village.

Tom only had to stop once to consult a map. I hadn't realized, at that stage, that Rome was so easy to find your way around. I hung on to Tom's strong singer's chest from which I now knew beautiful music soared, and watched the most beautiful buildings and ruins and piazzas and streets in the world float by. I wished the ride and the week would never end.

An enigma

Saturday, September 10, 5.00 a.m. I have neglected you, my journal. Five whole days without an entry, falling into the huge canopied bed, neglecting also my practice, the work I had intended to do on *Figaro.* Sightseeing is hard, exhausting work. On the train tomorrow I must make amends.

Notes I must make, reminders for later expansion . . .

Tuesday, especially: the catacombs, the gathering storm, her unspoken but transparent pleasure for my music, that drawn-out and unforgettable ride back to the village, Rome's ancient and dramatic shadows, water and light on stone.

The Sistine Chapel, the Michelangelo ceiling and Last Judgement impossible to appreciate, ruined by noisy tourists and the strident voices of polyglot guides. Ditto all of the Vatican and St Peter's and the Pantheon, and all the museums. I must come down again in the winter months for less frenzied viewing, if I can afford it.

Yet: Alex will have no such chance, not for some years; she has drunk Rome in with an evident and avid thirst for its splendours, conscious of her short stay. If I've grown used to, even blasé about Italianate riches, her innocent wonder has been like a breath of fresh air. Many times I caught her impulsively running her hand over a pillar, the drapery or sandalled foot of a statue, the hewn chips of a mosaic; lost her briefly in the crowds as I went on ahead before she had drunk her fill of something — a painted ceiling, a tapestry, a circular staircase, a shop window full of beautiful shoes — that particularly took her fancy.

Yet: lost in wonder, maybe. Naïve, no. Only fifteen, hardly! I know Italians of twenty who, apparently sophisticated, are more naïve than Alex. Apart from the interchange on religion, (surprising, usually a no-go area for Kiwis) I know little more about her than I did at the beginning of the week. That ill-judged but understandable blunder of attempting a kiss, upon feeling those superb small breasts hard up against my back, cost me dearly. I've been grateful for the useful European custom of kissing a woman's hand. We've talked of everything — Rome, Italy ancient and modern — and nothing — of anything personal. An ephemeral expedient friendship, is that *all?* She seems — unconscious of her striking appearance, despite, or perhaps because of, her simple style of dress; is it antipodean innocence or a calculated worldliness? I don't know. Behind that again, a coldness, a reserve, disconcerting. If I had translated all the compliments passed by shopkeepers and waiters, she'd have written me and ordinary Romans off as flatterers, fawners, and creeps. Despite the apparent honesty of insisting she pay her own way, that her favours were not to be bought, I cannot read her.

Except: my risk in giving her a fairly demanding recital Schumann, Mozart et al — did, surely, come off. I remember girlfriends at home who would have been, by such an intimate recital, embarrassed, nonplussed, or bored to tears. You can always tell, in such intimate space, whether your audience is captivated or merely being polite. Yesterday, I managed by pure luck to acquire two costly tickets for *Aida* tonight, my last in Rome. The weather has settled down, Rome is again basking in its usual golden light, a little less hot. I'm relieved our drenching on Tuesday didn't result in a chill or sore throat — I have lost ground to recover next week.

The thought of breaking the spell, of saying goodbye to Alessandra after the opera tonight has begun to disturb me, more deeply than I bargained for.

Seats at the opera

'The opera?' said Zoe from her sleepy Saturday morning bed. 'You poor *thing.* What opera?'

'*Aida.* About an Egyptian princess. She gets buried alive.'

'Gawd. What are you wearing?'

'Does it matter?'

'Course it matters. What else do you go for, and don't kid me it's the music. Little black dress, pearls, high heels, loads of eye make-up, knock 'em for dead. Wasted on Bulldog, though. Pity you haven't got a nice guy. In a tuxedo.'

If she thought I was going with Mrs Churchill, fine. As for the nice guy, little did she know! Not nice, but interesting.

'My black dress wouldn't go anywhere near you. Tell you what,' she said, sitting up in all her hair-curler greasy-face glory, 'borrow my off-the-shoulder black top, that should stretch around your great shoulders.'

'Thanks.'

'Only joking. Seriously . . .'

'It's outdoors, and I've got a perfectly good jacket-dress.' Her enthusiasm to help was a relief — lost with Tom in the back streets of the Trastevere for lunch on Thursday, I'd forgotten all about going to her event on Thursday afternoon, and had to invent a feeble excuse about a press interview. She wasn't impressed. She ended up tenth, not bad out of twenty-three, and jumped 5 foot 4¾ inches, half an inch off her best. Iolanda Balas had, she said glumly, jumped only five inches higher than anyone else — what could you expect of someone who was six foot tall with legs up to her earholes and who jumped like a man? — none of the eastern Europeans or Russians looked much like women at all. She was equally disgusted that she had ended up behind her Aussie rival, and that I'd not come to cheer her on.

To humour her, I put on the black top. It looked a bit strange with no bra and my pyjama bottoms. 'Pull the sleeves down. Lower. *Lower*. That looks great. With one of your better skirts, some earrings . . .'

'No thanks,' I said, though I'd been tempted by the slinky reflection in the mirror, my shoulders bold and bare. Would it knock Tom out, or would I merely feel embarrassed? Both, probably.

'Your funeral,' she said, lying back in bed. 'Be boring.'

I went training later than usual and met Tom outside the village gate at eleven, wearing the coral pink dress which had needed a good iron after the other night, with the bolero jacket and some court shoes in my bag. *This* time the weather looked perfect. I had strict instructions from Bulldog; straight home the minute the opera finished, in a taxi, and no hanky-panky, mind. She'd not sleep until I was back safely.

Outside the main entrance, Tom looked different again; he'd left off the moustache and was wearing normal clothes — light navy trousers, white shirt, panama hat; he could pass for English or a normal, boring Kiwi. We'd planned a quieter day, walking in the Villa Borghese, a long lunch, visiting a couple of the less touristy churches. From the Games village down the long stretch of the Via Flaminia to the Piazza del Popolo, plunging into the crowded Rome beyond — hitching my leg over the scooter, impervious to the traffic, to hooting cars and screeching tyres — I was beginning to feel like a real Roman moll.

Our late, long lunch in a rather swept-up ristorante near the Pincio started off unpromisingly. We both knew that time was running out. Sometime in the next three days he'd kiss my hand for the last time and we'd walk off in different directions.

'Tell me, Miss Alexandra Archer,' said Tom across the orange tablecloth. He picked up the tall pepperpot and held it out: a mike. The voice was rich, flat, monotonous American. 'Olympic bronze medallist, the only woman of the New Zealand team to win a medal. One of the youngest ever Olympic medallists in any sport, how do you feel, about to return back home to fame and glory? Tell the listeners Stateside, how will it feel?'

'According to you, it won't be much fun.' Tomorrow was the closing ceremony. Monday, I was off to Naples. I wasn't in any mood for games.

'Of course it will. At first,' he said, dropping the accent. 'Interviews at the airport, flash bulbs popping off, honour at school, family parties, showing everyone your slides. Presumably some public appearances, speeches to Rotary, prizegivings, Country Women's Institutes.'

'And then?'

He hailed the waiter and studied the menu, diversionary tactics. Now I knew what lire were worth compared to New Zealand pounds, I was shocked by the prices on the menu.

'I don't know why we came here,' I said.

'Being our last lunch, this one's on me,' he said.

'No it isn't. And why's it our last?'

'It would give me great pleasure.'

'But not me. I'd rather keep it down the middle. I'll have antipasti first and then the tortellini, thanks. E una birra.' I looked around the crowded ristorante as Tom did the ordering. The usual people were staring at his hair. At one table, two females in arty black clothes were almost nose to nose saying an intense goodbye, snarling softly at each other. One swept out, leaving the other staring at her red wine.

I said, 'You were going to tell me . . .'

'No I'm not. You don't need me to tell you it's going to be hard to settle down to training, school, family routine. Two months till accrediting exams.'

And afterwards, in December, playing Joan in three scenes from *Saint Joan*, one bright speck on the horizon. The beer arrived, pale gold in a tall frosty glass. I drank half straight off in one ice-cold sluice. So he knew all along I was only a sixth former, a schoolkid, a fraud.

'I don't even know what school you're at,' he said. 'You've been rather reticent about your life back home.'

'You also,' I shot back. There was an uneasy silence. 'Do you know what I miss here? The sea. Knowing it's close by, just a bike-ride away. I don't think I could live away from the sea.'

'We could have gone out to Anzio or Ostia. I think you'd have been disappointed, if you like beaches clean and uncrowded.'

'I'm looking forward to Naples.' I said, lying brightly.

'Alas, I'll be back in Milan. I have to catch a train in the morning.'

'I thought . . . aren't you coming to the closing ceremony?'

'I'm sorry if I gave you that impression. Much as I'd like to, I'm expected back on Monday. Which is why I've dispensed with Tommaso and Dennis the Aussie. They served their purpose. Shall we?' I followed him to the antipasto table, the most colourful array yet. At a nearby table, the abandoned woman in black was staring at us. Tom said, 'I've got to start regular practice again. I've Figaro and Marcello in *Bohème* to prepare, a Schubert and Schumann lieder recital. Some more arias, hopefully for an audition or two.'

'What for?' My plate was becoming rather full. 'What's that?'

'Calamari. Squid. Try it. Experience and practice, mainly, at this stage. To impress a conductor, a manager, an agent, anyone who might give me a small part somewhere.'

In other words, he's never coming back to New Zealand, not for ages, so what's the bloody point. As we took our loaded plates back to the table, I tried to sound casual, not too eager.

'Couldn't you come tomorrow night, go back on Monday? Fly or something.'

Half of me recognized the shake of the head. It was the shake of someone locked into their own private system of what they'd set themselves to do, no compromises for girlfriends, flu, or anything else. The other half of me said, if he was really serious, he'd give up *one* day of silly old exercises and arias, and come with me to Naples.

'Mi scusi.' At first I thought it must be some Italian friend of Tom's. Then I recognized the abandoned woman in black. She was standing over us, swaying slightly on very high, black heels, with her handbag tucked under her arm, a full bottle of red wine in one hand and a glass in the other. 'Please, I think you are English.'

'Yes,' said Tom.

'I would like so much to join you. May I . . .' She didn't wait for the answer. A passing waiter was ordered to bring her chair.

I thought it was a bit of a nerve just interrupting complete strangers, and people half your age at that. She was at least forty, with lots of bangles, black hair carelessly back-combed up to the sky. Her face was drawn on: black cat's eyes like Sophia Loren, but smudged, more rouge on one side than the other, all except the outline of her lipstick worn off. She was smiling at me, very friendly.

'I hear you speak of Marcello in *Bohème*. . . you are a sing-ger, un baritono?' she said, turning to Tom. Her voice was deep, like gravel on a beach.

'Not me,' he said smiling, the voice of a BBC announcer. 'We're English. I'm an accountant, and I know absolutely nothing about opera. I have a musical second cousin who is playing the role at Covent Garden next season.'

'Ah, Covent Garden. But I hear you say . . .'

'You must have been mistaken,' he said politely. She poured herself a full glass of wine, and refused to take no for an answer when Tom said we didn't drink red wine in the middle of the day. Glasses were summoned and filled, another bottle ordered. Tom and I began our antipasto. She watched us with her painted cat's eyes from above the glass of wine.

'Such a handsome couple. The one so bless-ed,' she gestured at Tom's hair, 'the other so fresh and young. I think you are an athlete, my dear?'

'My sister is a well-known tennis player in England,' said Tom before I could open my mouth. 'Next season she will play at Wimbledon.'

This could have been quite funny, except that our friend was in rather a bad way. Her voice was slow and slurred, her hands shook slightly, her mouth smiled but her eyes stared. I had never seen a woman who you might call an alcoholic. There was something else too.

'You English, so obsessed with sport. ' 'Ere it is music, l'opera.' Her gravelly voice took on a sing-song lilt. 'Venezia. Roma, Trieste, Spoleto, Palermo, Firenze — I 'ave sung in them all. Verdi, Puccini, Donizetti, Rossini, Mozart, Gluck, Bellini, Offenbach, Mascagni, Leoncavallo I 'ave sung.'

'You're lucky,' said Tom.

'Not lucky,' she flashed. 'Hard work. You don't know who I am.'

'Should we?' said Tom smiling carefully. She had not told us her name.

'Many great mezzo roles I 'ave sung,' she said sadly, rattling off the names of a good many, and where she sang them, and with which conductor. As we ate our tortellini, she informed us that a growth on her vocal chords six years ago had finished her career as a soloist. Operations and what the doctors said about nodules the size of marbles didn't go too well with the tortellini.

So, she had retired. Now she sang, she said, only occasionally, a little chorus work, some teaching. Her friend sang with the opera in Rome, she was a soprano, but her friend had left, she had been so cruel, so very cruel, she had left.

'Let me get you a taxi,' said Tom suddenly.

'Your friend understands, he is so sweet,' she said to me. 'You have Diana's arms, so strong, powerful, so beautiful,' and to my horror she ran her hand up and down my upper arm. Her hand was hot and not smooth. Then — swiftly, before I could move away — down one side of my face. By this time Tom was at the back of her chair.

'I've called a taxi,' he said in her ear. 'Stay there, Alex, order a pud, this may take a while.' He virtually pulled her off the chair. There was a three-way uproar in Italian, bringing in the waiter, which started at our table and continued at the desk by the door. I guessed it involved her bill, her outrage at not being allowed to take away a nearly full bottle of wine. By this time everyone was looking. Eventually Tom escorted her out the main entrance. Another ten minutes went by before he returned. The waiter must have decided I was bored and a soft touch for pudding. He trundled over a trolley of the most fantastic rich-looking cakes and glistening fruit tarts, and to pass the time I chose a monstrous piece of a torte absolutely smothered in almonds and chocolate flakes and cream and ordered un caffè.

'What does she do for an encore?' I said. I could still feel her fingers on my cheekbones. I wasn't quite sure why it had made my skin crawl so.

Tom gave me a searching look, then ordered a coffee from the hovering waiter.

'Have some cake,' I said. 'Fantastic.'

'No thanks.'

'Does that sort of thing happen often?'

'In big cities, yes. Desperate people, lonely as hell. She knew she couldn't pay the bill. Her lover went off . . .'

'But she was with a woman.'

Tom shrugged. 'Takes all sorts. Italians are generally more relaxed about such things. Her own word — lovers, amante, she said, for four years, today finished. She must have been very good, once. Only the best get to sing big roles like Amneris in *Aida* and the gypsy Azucena in *Trovatore*.'

In other words, that's how you end up if you get nodules on your vocal chords or for whatever reason don't last the distance: alcoholic and lonely and scrounging help from tourists in restaurants. 'Did you help her, with the bill?'

'Some.' He smiled, ruefully. 'You could call it insurance money.'

'I'll shout you a piece of cake, cheer you up.'

'Alright, since it's our last. Thank you, Alex,' he said, surprisingly. He chose a large, flat piece of raspberry tart, and ordered some gorgonzola for us to share as well. It was getting on for four o'clock. Tonight we'd get caught up in the opera. I decided it was as good an opportunity as any for some straight talking.

'What time is your train in the morning?'

'9.30, I think.'

'I'm sorry you're not staying for the closing ceremony. Perhaps I could send you a postcard.'

He smiled. 'I'm sorry you're not coming to Milan. Perhaps I could send *you* a postcard.'

We formally got out our diaries and swopped addresses, mine in Auckland, his in Milan, care of a family called Bargellini.

'If you're ever back in Auckland . . .' I said.

Aida was everything I imagined and hoped for, though I was close to tears all night. We arrived early, before dusk, and wandered round the ruins, admiring the archways and the green and white mosaic floors, the small, flat, perfect bricks they'd made so long ago. Slowly the crowds arrived, the light began to fade from blue to streaky orange to black. We found our fantastic seats on the huge temporary stand, right in the middle, facing the stage between the two highest towers of the ruins. Nothing would persuade him to let me pay for my ticket. It was a prize for doing so well, he said, a small gesture from a proud expatriate. With his white shirt, a lightweight tweed jacket, a hat which he took off as the lights went down, I thought this was about as close to the real Tom as I was going to get. The night was still, the trees around all floodlit in blue. I felt like a five-year-old at her first pantomime.

The music really was only half of it. The sheer size of everything took my breath away — the orchestra, the Egyptian scenery, the stage itself, the chorus, the march with horses and camels, the strapping soprano who was Aida, and the even larger tenor who was Radames. Tom sat in his seat through the whole three hours like someone electrified, and was one of the first on his feet after the final terrible chords with the two lovers waiting to die in the tomb. Bravo! we shouted happily, along with everyone else.

I think we'd already started to pull apart, as we drifted out of the ruins, found the bike, and started on the return journey. It was after midnight. He didn't suggest a last drink or gelato, even if you could get one that late. He drove slowly, three times round the Colosseum, a detour to the Trevi Fountain, twice around the Piazza del Popolo, and a detour into part of the Borghese gardens. He sang all the way, some songs I knew like 'They're Changing Guard at Buckingham Palace' and 'Three Coins in the Fountain', and 'Some Enchanted Evening', and even my favourite Maori songs 'E hine e' and 'Pokare kare ana' (which surprised me from someone who didn't have anything good to say about New Zealand). Not loudly, but I could feel the resonance vibrating in his solid warm back.

It was 1.30 when we arrived at the village. At the gate, things got awkward, as I knew they would. I got off the bike and stood looking down. He had not had a hat on for hours now. The amazing hair glowed in the lamplight.

'You never did give me a driving lesson,' I said.

'We forgot. Too many other things.'

'Thanks for the opera. Everything.'

'It's been a great week. Thank *you*.'

It's up to you, kissing-wise he had said, six days ago. He'd stuck to his side of the bargain. My heart was bursting, but I just couldn't move. We should have done it earlier, if at all. He broke the terrible silence by leaning forward, taking my hand and bestowing a last kiss, lingering, as they say in those soppy serials. He *lingered*.

'G'night Kiwi. Take care. Have a good flight home.'

'I will.' I heard him say something in Italian. Then I couldn't stand it any more. 'Thanks again,' I said, walking quickly past the guard. I didn't look back, because I had tears in my eyes and couldn't have seen anything anyway.

After I reported to Bulldog, I spent the rest of the night on the roof.

Sunday September 11. Slept late (three hours sleep), went training late, last time in my beautiful bronze pool. Keep thinking about America next year. If I go to Aussie in January, they'll expect me to beat Dawn Fraser, if she's still swimming, if I'm still swimming, if . . .

Bulldog is annoying me, making pointed comments about keeping her awake last night. Haven't told her that T. has gone, caught a bloody train, gone back to his beloved Milan and his beloved singing. Music at closing ceremony tonight best part, that and when they put the Olympic flame out. Stadium went dark, and then someone lit a small flame, probably their programme, and then the idea spread and the whole stadium lit with tiny pinpricks of fire, pure magic. Teams all sitting together in stands, not on field, only flags paraded there. Tears, for various reasons. Then fantastic fireworks and choir and orchestra belting out something operatic, programme said 'Hymn to the Sun' by Mascagni from an opera called *Iris*, ended on repeated high note, cymbal crashes, the works. I'm giving up opera.

Monday September 12. Train this morning to Naples — me, Mr U, and Bulldog. SAW THE SEA. In the distance, not very often. Longer trip than expected, mostly inland, train crowded. What coastline we did see, so *pretty*, houses on rocky hillsides, fishing villages in little coves, boats. Naples huge, smoky, quite different colours to Rome, yellows, whites, blues, the bluest SEA absolutely ever. Taxi to hotel, view of the famous harbour, and Mount Vesuvius, palm trees, more tropical feel than Rome. Found a trattoria, Bulldog and Mr U *hopeless.* Haven't learnt a thing. Couldn't be bothered telling them what calamari were, or fragole. Tired. Lonely. Want to go home. Period coming? Have I been away a month?

Tuesday September 13. Swam this morning in pool, old-fashioned place, lots of pillars. Most top swimmers here, including Aussies. Kept my distance, still uncomfortable, odd. Rest in afternoon, very hot. Want to go for swim in sea, BADLY. Carnival a washout, packed stands but most swimmers just going through motions, joke. Swam in 200 metres, felt dreadful, period still coming, lousy time, came fourth. Dawn Fraser didn't finish for some reason — maybe got mouthful or cramp, looked upset later. Can't imagine why I bothered to keep training. WANT TO GO HOME.

Wednesday September 14. Day sightseeing, bus along famous waterfront, fishing boats and castles and enticing boat trips to Capri and Ischia. Bulldog and Mr U wanted to go to Pompeii instead, so we went to Pompeii. Glad, though, fantastic view of whole bay, amazing ruins, roadways with grooves for sewerage, baker shops with actual ovens and millstones, atrium houses, temples. Some horrible plaster bodies: people smothered by the eruption, a dog with its feet in the air. They filled in the spaces left when the bodies had decomposed, and got these awful impressions of what it was like. Clever guide spoke in English, French, Italian and German. Adored the paintings, that beautiful soft red. Some rude paintings only men allowed to go and see. Women hung about feeling stupid, Mr U and other men went, came back red in face, wouldn't say what they saw. Guidebook says they show couples, being erotic. Takes two to tango. Nowhere to swim in sea, no beaches, no sand, couldn't stop in bus anyway. Want to swim in sea, so BADLY. Naples overrated. Washing hanging out of windows and poor kids in streets.

Caught night train back to Rome. Period arrived. Joined up with rest of team in hotel, near airport. Could be anywhere. Daren't think of the Colosseum, the pool, the village, the river, the bridge, so familiar, so near yet so far. Only memories. My three races, dancing a minuet on the concourse, seeing my flag go up. The pink trattoria after St Peter's, the room with the harp where he sang Schubert and 'How Sweet to be a Cloud', the Colosseum after the storm. Dancing naked under the moon on the roof. Want to scream. Can't sleep. Writing this 3 a.m. Going home today, same way as we came.

They still had the Olympic flags flying at the airport, but no bands, no buzz.

We had half an hour to wait after checking in our bags. Bulldog wanted to buy some last minute presents, and Zoe was off with her athletic mates. I couldn't bear the thought of either the airport shops or sitting down. We had five *days* of that ahead. I wandered over to a window where I could see the planes, ours with TEAL written on the tail, fuel tankers around it and men in overalls with clipboards and earmuffs. There was no colour in the scene — just grey concrete, grey planes, grey grass, hazy, bleached-looking sky, grey hazy Rome in the distance. Suited just how I felt, washed out, my uniform scruffy already. My hair needed cutting and I'd got badly sunburnt on my shoulders walking around Pompeii in a sleeveless dress. I had a bronze medal in my handbag and a huge hole where my heart should have been . . .

Five minutes to go, five days cooped up in a tin tube. I turned around to look at the departure lounge. Our men were standing around in bored groups, their cabin bags between their feet. European-looking people came and went through the swing doors, smart women travelling in high heels, trailing porters with sets of baggage, men in suits, men in bright shirts. One erupted through the doors, took a wild look around, and started walking over to me. It couldn't be. He was in Milan, for ever.

'I thought I was going to miss you,' he said, stopping two feet away, his powerful chest heaving, and in a split-second decision, deciding to be a devil and give me the Italian-style double hug. 'Some fool of a girl at the Embassy told me the wrong time. I wanted to be here earlier, when you arrived.'

'Did you fly?'

'Hitched. Long-distance truck down the autostrada, nearly six hundred kilometres. I left at dawn.'

'Just to say goodbye?'

He didn't deny it. He was wearing the same clothes as our *Aida* night, except for the Italian straw boater. With the team around — Tom or Tommaso? I was feeling exhilaration and anger, in about equal parts.

'Well,' I said, 'can I ask why you bothered, when I'm about to get on a plane for New Zealand and you're about to go back to some gorgeous Italian opera-singing girlfriend who's about to sing Madame Butterfly?'

'I don't have one of those,' he said, exasperated, taking his hat off. 'I just wanted to say, oh how much I've wanted to say.'

'Like?'

'Like — oh, God, thank you for that wonderful week, Rome illuminated by your . . .'

'Cut it out!'

'It's so easy to get blasé in Europe. Look, I just wanted to tell you, I don't know when I'll be back in New Zealand, but . . .'

'Never, from the sound of it.'

'That's what I said when I left home. The whole place was beginning to appall me.'

'Why?'

'Too many reasons . . . this is not the time and place.'

'I'm interested.'

'In a nutshell, the feeling of suffocation, the hypocrisy of a small, boring, humourless, unmusical, and generally cultureless desert run by small, boring people obsessed with sport, philistines to a man.'

Behind him I could see Mr Upjohn wave, and a general bestirring of the team near him.

'I don't agree and I think that's our . . .' I began.

'No, listen. I've been thinking . . . I might be . . .'

'Tom, at the risk of presuming rather a lot' — I heard an echo from a lunch somewhere, 'don't you *ever* come back to New Zealand for a woman. She's not worth it.' Mr Upjohn was on his fat way over.

'If I come back next year it wouldn't . . . '

'She doesn't want the responsibility, when you find out what an ambitious bitch she is and it all goes wrong.'

150

'I'm not giving her that responsibility. I swore I wouldn't go back to New Zealand except . . .'

'Alex?' Mr Upjohn had arrived. I could see his eyes on Tom's extraordinary hair. 'Excuse me but . . . gracious, it's Tommaso, our interpreter, without his hat.' He couldn't quite bring himself to say anything about hair; Kiwi blokes don't talk about personal things like hair in public. 'We thought you'd gone back to Milan. You were immensely helpful.'

'My name is Tom Alexander, Mr Upjohn. I'm actually a Kiwi, living in Milan.'

'But you speak Italian!'

'It is possible to be both a Kiwi and speak Italian.' The gentle sarcasm was utterly lost on Mr Upjohn. 'I'm studying here. Tommaso was a rather prolonged but I hope quite helpful joke.'

I noticed he didn't explain or apologize, as such. I saw Mr Upjohn's eyes go cold. He turned to me. 'Mrs Churchill told me you'd been sightseeing all last week with a cousin, nephew of a Christchurch city councillor, a Tom Alexander in whom she had complete confidence. Is this him?'

'Yes,' I said. She must have added the cousin bit for extra reassurance.

'I do not appreciate being made to look foolish, Alex,' he said. 'Presumably you knew about this charade.'

I couldn't help smiling. 'Oh yes.'

'And Mrs Churchill?'

'Well, um . . .' I couldn't lie quick enough. Mr Upjohn shot Tom a look of intense dislike. 'Excuse me, Mr Alexander, but our flight has been called.'

'Of course,' said Tom evenly. Mr Upjohn led off. 'Believe me now?' he muttered, putting his hat back on. I could see what was going to happen. Others, straggling towards the departure gate, recognized him. Tommaso! they cried, genuinely pleased to see him again.

I think Tom had arrived determined to come clean with the whole team, but pompous old Mr Uphimself had run true to form. There just wasn't time to explain and enjoy the joke. So he was stuck with Tommaso. They shook his hand and cried Arrivederci, grazie, Tommaso, and Tom shrugging helplessly for once, slipped back into his stage Italian English. I straggled to the end of the team, with Mr Upjohn sticking to me like a leech, until we were the last three.

'Arrivederci Tommaso,' I said. 'Grazie tanto per la bellissima settimana.' It probably wasn't grammatical, but who cared. Mr Upjohn's eyes popped out of his head.

'Prego, Alessandra la bella, la più coraggiosa,' Tom said, with a desperate, defeated look in his brown eyes. 'Remember me to Auckland. Oh, and greetings to Marcia Macrae.'

'Who?'

'Isn't she one of your teachers?'

'Oh, Miss Macrae, yes. What's the connection?'

'Alex, we must go,' said Mr Upjohn.

'She and my mother were at drama school in London together, before the war. She wrote to me about you coming to Rome.'

'So this whole thing was jacked up by Miss Macrae?'

'Not jacked up,' he said, beginning to realize his mistake. 'A helpful gesture, that's all.'

'Am I sick of helpful gestures. People organizing my life for me, even ten thousand miles away.'

'Alex?' said Mr Upjohn.

'I'm *coming.*' I was feeling ill with disappointment. It had been my first ever true week of freedom, the two of us completely free from people pulling strings; or so I'd thought. 'So we were dancing to Miss Macrae's and your mother's tune, were we?'

'My mother's been dead for years, and no we weren't. Oh God, how do I convince you, her letter only came during the week, after . . .'

'Alex!!' Mr Upjohn, agitato.

' . . . after we'd met at the Colosseum, even that wasn't the first time I . . .' In a mixture of anger and defiance and bloodymindedness and mischief, I took off his hat and kissed him full on the mouth, stopping any more words coming out. It was brief, beautiful, and final. I shut my eyes and thought: 2.5 seconds can be a long, long time, ask any swimmer. Put that in your pipe, Mr Upyourself, angry with the both of us, and Tom, who'd hitchhiked on a truck all the way from Milan but just spoiled everything. I had nothing to lose. I'd lost him already. I'd never see him again.

'Ciao, Tommaso, Tom, whoever you are,' I said. I put his hat back on, took a last look at the face I'd thought I'd got to know rather well, and the startled brown eyes, and walked blindly through the gate. The beautiful voice followed me.

'Ciao, Alessandra.'

Sweet sorrow

I am left staring at a grey screen just inside a gaping doorway framed by two uniformed and interested guards. They, not hearing all that ridiculous carry-on with the men of the team — 'Molto grazie, Tommaso, ciao', their ten words of local lingo, with me bowing and scraping 'prego, prego signor' — and assuming I am English, exchange some lewd comments pertaining to Alex's height and long legs, to certain rumours coming out of the Olympic village regarding the athletes, those perfect bodies coupling, to the happy abundance in Rome this summer of free-wheeling girls. I tell them coarsely to keep their filthy tongues to themselves, provoking an accusation from one: hadn't the tall girl just shown me she was in love? why was I, an Italian, letting her go? what was wrong with me . . .?

They and the empty doorway mock me. An Italian — the irony of it. I'd certainly not get past them. The powerful urge to let fly with a straight hook, to wipe off that knowing Latin smile, would result only in being removed by airport security. I walk away.

I can smell something sharp — the stick of 4711 eau de cologne I've seen her use? My mouth tastes faintly of lemon. Tom, thou *fool*.

I can see the plane marked TEAL, maybe a hundred and fifty yards away. Technicians and trucks still work alongside; something that looks like a movie camera is set up by the gangway, but as yet no passengers are walking out from the final departure area. I rest my forehead on the glass, one arm curved above my head, and watch tears form in ragged black circles on the concrete floor.

Nineteen months in Italy, nary a twinge of homesickness for

155

a country without passion, history, warmth, or generosity; bleak, raw, mean, Victorian, materialistic, and suspicious . . .

Till now, when I'd sell my soul to be getting on that plane. To fly in five days' time over the rugged western coastline, over the beaches where I've dug toheroa from the black sand, over the green farmlands and orchards and inlets of water surrounding Auckland, to walk under the oaks in Princes Street or along the sands of Takapuna after a ferry ride across the harbour. I forget: the bridge has been completed. She lives in Epsom, near One Tree Hill, Cornwall Park with its avenue of olive trees . . .

The loudspeaker is playing that banal and infernal song again. 'Arrivederci Roma, it's time for us to part . . .'

It's forty long minutes before I see the first passengers straggle unwillingly across the tarmac, about half of them carrying black blazers. Several people have materialized around the camera, and are filming their departure. She comes among the last, with Mrs Churchill, head erect, never looking back.

She is laughing?

She can forget me, my six hundred kilometre journey to see her, even that wretched last conversation, so quickly, easily? If I, if our Olympic time meant anything at all . . . Alessandra, are you so self-contained, so hard? Alessandra!

At the foot of the gangway, then standing at the open doorway into the plane, she is being filmed. The film star's wave, posed, contrived, trite, no doubt required of her. But even from here (curse my long sight) she looks extraordinarily happy to be leaving. Perhaps she is? Or an act? She laughs at the camera crew below, looks once briefly at the airport buildings (did she think I might still be here, watching?) and vanishes.

I see the door close, the plane fire up its four propellers, move slowly away, taxi to the end of the runway, and take off to the south. The wheels go up. It's soon gone, into low grey cloud. I feel anger, disenchantment; utterly desolate.

Melodramatic, perhaps, but I need to sing of my pain to forget that dumb show of farewell, to strangers, forget those grey disappointed eyes, that lemon-tasting kiss. Private music to express what words alone cannot.

Parting is not such sweet sorrow. It's the price of ambition. It's a reminder of why I choose to stay here, why I must forget

Alessandra, Rome, the whole bitter-sweet Olympics, why Maestro will be waiting for me at ten o'clock tomorrow morning.

I wander outside and begin to walk back to Milan.

Arrivederci Roma

'My dear, but we don't mind tears at all,' says the dark-haired interviewer dressed in best British tweeds and an old school tie. 'Arrivederci Roma' comes clearly out of the loudspeakers. 'The music is exactly right, too, as we requested. If you will just . . . over here.'

I shake off the hand which is cupped around my elbow, about to steer me in the direction of a camera and lights set up in a corner alcove of the departure lounge. 'No,' I say again, the tears still rolling. And I am sick to bloody death of that song!

'Alex, you'll do as you're asked,' mutters Mr Upjohn behind me, angrily. 'This is a British television crew, making a documentary programme on the Games.'

'If you knew they'd be here, why didn't you give me any warning?'

'I hardly got a chance, you and that bogus young red-head. I shall protest to Mrs Churchill in the strongest possible terms.'

'Why? He didn't do you any harm, he just showed me round Rome — we saw lots of things, I learnt lots, a perfect gentleman . . .'

'I knew there was something odd about him . . .'

'And just what . . ?'

'Mr Upjohn,' said the interviewer smoothly, 'Excuse me, I'm sorry, but we don't have a great deal of time, maybe twenty minutes before your final call.'

Behind him, as he speaks, I see Mrs Churchill searching through the crowd of people standing around. She spies us and comes bustling over. Close behind her comes Norm Thompson, hat pushed to the back of his head, notebook in hand, looking creased and worn-out.

159

'Alex, dear, where did you get to?' she cries.

'I was saying goodbye to Tom.'

'Yes, I shall have something further to say to you, Enid, on that score,' says Mr Upjohn.

'The cat out of the bag?' Bulldog asks me, smiling.

I nod, also smiling through my tears, to Mr Upjohn's fury. His eyes fall on Norm Thompson's face.

'Norm, did you know about this, too?' he demands.

'Miss Archer, please?' says the interviewer.

'Alright,' I say, because anything will be better than this stupid conversation. Who cares? Tom played a lengthy trick on them, all clean fun, so what? He is on the other side of that screen, he isn't worth worrying about any more. 'Lead on. But no sloppy tears,' I say, sniffing hard as we walk towards the lights.

'Has Rome been the city of romance, then?' he says archly. He is boringly tall dark n' handsome, at a guess a bit older than Tom, as BBC and smooth-tongued as they come.

'No, it hasn't, and please don't ask me anything about boyfriends and men 'cause I won't answer, there's nothing to tell anyway and have you got a handkerchief?'

'Of course.' It's Irish linen, unused. 'Keep it. My name's Michael Harrington-Jones, by the way. I'm so pleased to meet you.'

'Thanks.' I blow my nose as I see two chairs, one with a microphone on it, set out under the lights, and realize what I am letting myself in for. 'How come you got permission to be here?'

'We simply asked. We wanted the youngest Olympic medallist before she flew home to fame and glory. Sit here, make yourself comfortable. The proximity is necessary, I'm afraid, for the small screen. May I call you Alex?' He has picked up the microphone on its stalk and consulted a clipboard, and is looking at the girl and five men dressed in jeans behind the camera, waiting for the signal to start. We are uncomfortably close, our knees practically touching. 'Derek, get them to turn that music down a bit. Now, Alex, just relax, don't be nervous.'

'I'm not. Hell's bells,' I say, recoiling as someone thrusts another light practically into my face, blinding me.

160

'Sorry about the sun gun. You'll get used to it. Your first time in front of a camera?'

'No,' I lie, swiping the hanky across my nose and eyes again.

'Good. I'm very friendly, I won't bite you. Ready? We've adjusted the sound for all this noise, but try to speak up clearly.' After a long pause he must have got a signal. I still couldn't see anything but lights, glaringly white.

The microphone goes back and forth between us. I keep wanting to lean back, put a more comfortable space between us so that I can't see the gold fillings in his front teeth, but of course I can't, there's nowhere to go. Trapped!

'Alex Archer, you came to Rome a completely unknown young swimmer from New Zealand. You're going home with a bronze medal in your pocket, the youngest competitor of the Games to win a medal.'

'I still can't believe it.'

'How did you feel, standing on the victory dais with Fraser and Von Saltza?'

'Sort of numb. I don't remember much at all.'

'You were so overcome?'

'I must've been. I do remember the spotlight on the flags going up, all red white and blue — and grinning like a Cheshire Cat. Dawn Fraser wearing a white track suit and waving her koala bear around, all the Aussies screaming Dawnie.' (I remember being utterly aware of Tom in the shadows nearby, several times meeting his smiling eyes.)

'Dawn Fraser's your heroine, obviously.'

'I think she's amazing. She knew who I was even before the heats.'

'How many years of training has it taken, to stand on that dais?'

'About five or six. All through this winter at home. It's winter there now.'

'So I believe. But how was it possible, coming from virtually no competition in New Zealand to an Olympic bronze?'

'I had plenty of competition. A certain girl called Maggie Benton, for years.'

'A famous rivalry, in New Zealand?'

161

'I don't know about famous. She usually won, up till last summer.'

'So you won the place in the Olympic team?'

'We both got in. But she got peritonitis just before we left. She should have been here too.'

'How do you think she would have swum?'

'I've no idea.' (Yes I have, I think her mother would have made life impossible for both of us, and neither of us would have got past the heats.) 'I think she'd have done well. I never beat her easily.'

'What will it be like, getting off the plane in New Zealand?'

'After five days of sitting bolt upright, wonderful.'

'I mean the reaction to your medal?'

'They'll say, not bad, kiddo.'

'You don't mean to say that literally. Surely, that's a New Zealand expression for . . .'

'Flabbergasted. Amazed. Pulled a swiftie.'

'By that, do you mean a swift one, a fluke? But surely it wasn't a fluke, was it? Your times improved with each race.'

'Yes, they did, actually. But no one was more surprised than me.'

'Gold in Tokyo?'

'That's too far ahead.'

'People are saying that you look set to take over Dawn Fraser's world sprint crown when she retires.'

'Are they? I don't know about that. She hasn't said anything about retiring, has she?'

'They're saying you have the same degree of killer instinct necessary to win races.'

'I like to win, 'course I do. But killer instinct — I hate that expression, sounds like you're a shark, eating people. I don't eat people. I think I'm more a dolphin. I think I was a dolphin once. I bet, if I looked it up, dolphins swim faster than sharks.'

'I believe there is a possibility of an American swimming scholarship next year?'

'There's lots of possibilities for next year.' (How do people find out these things? Mr Upjohn?)

'Such as?'

'It's too soon. I haven't decided. Maybe swim in Australia.'
(Oops, is that a state secret?) 'Last year at school, probably.'

'And then?'

'I want to study law.'

'So you couldn't accept the American offer?'

'I didn't say that. I just said I wanted to study law, somewhere, sometime.'

'I imagine you were quite a grown-up young woman before you came to Rome, Alex.'

'I think that sounds a bit patronizing.'

'I'll rephrase that question. What do you think coming to Rome and doing so well at the Olympics, so surprisingly well, has done for you personally?'

(Gulp) 'Well, I've met lots of fantastic people. The Olympic ceremonies, I'll never forget those, the boy with the torch and the little fires at the closing ceremony. Or Rome, of course.'

'The Spanish steps, the Colosseum, the Catacombs . . . of course, to a New Zealander . . .'

'I don't think it matters where you come from, it's still fantastic. Learning all that Latin and ancient history seems to have some point, now.'

'Your impressions of the Olympic village?'

'Well, mostly it was great, everyone in together, people from all different sports, all different colours. Tho' the women's quarters were a bit like being in prison. Guards with guns, truly. And having to eat with the South Africans.'

'Tricky, you mean, because of the rugby series being played? Which they won?'

'I mean because I don't like the idea of apartheid, and our rugby team shouldn't have gone at all.' (Ohmigawd, here we go again.)

'Alex, would you show us your bronze medal?' His voice changes. 'Take your time. We edit the film, of course. I really don't want to get into politics, m'dear. My apologies, I meant to ask you earlier to have your medal ready.'

I get the box out of my handbag, relieved to have a break from our knees touching and looking into his staring blue eyes and gold fillings. I don't much want to get onto politics for British television either. I am beginning to wonder which is worse, interviewers who try to trip you up, or those who flatter you to the skies, or those who do both, like this one. I drape the chain of leaves over my hand. Under the harsh lights the burnished bronze perfectly matches the miniature that hangs on the bracelet around my wrist. To my dismay, I feel my eyes grow moist, and things happen at the back of my throat.

'Would you hold it a little higher, Alex? It was all worthwhile, do you think, all those years, all that winter training?'

'Yes, of course it was.' (I am swallowing. How do you stop tears? Will-power? I will not cry. I will not cry.)

'And Roma, la Città Eterna, the city of music, opera, song, and romance? Wonderful memories for a beautiful young woman to take home?'

'Yes, wonderful.' (A flatterer — what's that lovely word — sycophant, and turning out to be sneaky too, and my will-power pathetic and eyes now full of water and no doubt glistening and very obvious to the man holding the light in my face.)

'Romantic memories?'

'Lots.'

'And when you get off the plane in Auckland, a New Zealand national sporting heroine?'

'No, I'm no different, I'm not a heroine, never will be. I'm just me. Look, I'll have to stop this because I'm beginning to talk like a parrot and say things I don't mean and I'm going to cry again, and you must have other people you want to interview.'

I put the medal back into the box, coiling the chain into place, and stand up, knocking against his well-tailored knees and tripping over the microphone cord. 'I'm sorry, it was my first time with a camera and I'm no good at witty, pithy quotes, and don't use that last bit, please.'

Michael Harrington-Jones stands up too. 'But you were splendid, Alex, splendid,' he says untruthfully. 'Just what we wanted. I shall follow your career with great interest. You've a fine future in front of you, I'm sure.'

'I've got five days in an aeroplane, assuming we make it,' I say through my tears. 'Coming over, the wheels got stuck, coming into Karachi.'

'How very alarming.' We both listen to an announcement: our flight being called. 'When you go out to the aircraft, we've got a camera set up by the gangway. Will you give the camera some happy or tearful waves, whatever, we don't mind.'

Posing like ruddy film stars do for newsreels, I think, as I escape from much handshaking, many thank yous, good luck, happy landings with all seven of them. In the toilet, my eyes look a mess, I look a mess, the film will look terrible, and I have just gone on record as an uncouth kid from the colonies. When I come out, the first people are walking out to the plane. I wonder if Tom is already on his way back to Milan, or if he's still waiting, watching out of a window. He loathes airports. So do I, now.

Happy or tearful? In a funny, complicated sort of way, I'm both. I'm still angry, but I'm going home, and I have to admit listening to Michael Harrington-Jones carry on about me 'taking over Dawn Fraser's world sprint crown', though crazy and scary, has done wonders for my very weird state of mind.

So, happy it is, the best performance I can muster, in case . . . Walking out to the plane, Bulldog telling me about her ticking-off from Mr Upjohn while I was being interviewed, and I am certainly laughing. I wave happily to the camera at the foot of the steps, and again from the top. I look once over towards where people are crowding at the windows of what I think is the main departure hall, but my eyes aren't that good, and I can only see a blur of figures, no one special.

The plane is stuffy already, our seats cramped, Bulldog's fear of flying after the Karachi episode has made her not nice to be near, and this is only the beginning. The take-off is noisy and bumpy, the airport below a conglomeration of dull buildings and parked aeroplanes, and my ears are popping already.

Flying through the low cloud, while the terrified Bulldog beside me still has her eyes closed tight, I get out my bronze medal and stare at it in total wonderment.

I'm shivering slightly, though it's anything but cold. I rock my hand slowly back and forth to catch golden-red glints of light on the engraved figure of the athlete victorious, on my name, on the name of my country, cut in formal Roman lettering on the other side, on the thin leaves of beaten bronze.

When we came in to land, five weeks ago, I didn't even know if I could swim at the Olympics. Now, I hold this beautiful heavy burnished thing in my palm and I know damn well I'm going home to a whole lot of fame and glory. Only woman medallist of our team, youngest of the whole Games, et cetera. For a few days — alright, even a few weeks, off and on.

They'll clip your wings when you get home . . .

For the rest of my life, I'll always be Alex Archer, the Olympic bronze medallist. An Olympic medal — that was what any athlete wanted, more than anything else.

Wasn't it?

We are banking, altering course, I suppose for the first stop, Cairo. Suddenly we fly out of the cloud, into pure blue sky. The afternoon sun shines straight in my window. Looking down, through shreds of cloud, I can see the coastline against a sea so blue it makes my heart ache. On my hand the medal catches the sunlight, the athlete gleams intense coppery fire. He's so bright I have to shut my eyes.